Flyer

by

J L Wilson

The Remembered Classics Series

Flyer

Cover Art by *Kim Mendoza*

The Wild Rose Press, Inc.
PO Box 708
Adams Basin, NY 14410-0708
Visit us at www.thewildrosepress.com

Publishing History
First Crimson Rose Edition, 2018
Print ISBN 978-1-5092-1913-1
Digital ISBN 978-1-5092-1914-8

The Remembered Classics Series
Published in the United States of America

"What brings you back to town?"

"You." He looked down at me. "I wanted to be with you for the funeral." As always, he was simple, direct, and to the point.

"Thank you." I leaned against him, his comforting warmth an antidote to the sudden chill that made me shiver. "Where are you staying?"

He laughed softly. "Didn't you know? I'm a major stakeholder in that new motel they built out by the hospital. I had a suite built there for me."

The "new" two-story Kensington Arms Motel was built ten years before on the west side of town, just six blocks away from Mom's house. It was a significant improvement over the old ten-room roadside motel that had served travelers for half a century. "I'm sure it's not the Ritz or the Savoy," I said, moving away from him. A suite at the Kensington was probably two cramped rooms with a whirlpool tub in the john.

His eyes narrowed at my jibe. "It's clean, quiet, and private. That's all I really need."

"Not according to the magazine stories I've read about you." I walked past Peter's grave to the edge of the bluff. An oak tree, probably a hundred years old, towered over me. It was just losing its leaves to new spring growth and the lawn underneath was strewn with brown detritus. "You're a celebrity, Bell. It seems like you flit from hot spot to hot spot, always with the most beautiful people. You're the most eligible bachelor in the world."

He joined me on the bluff. "Don't believe everything you read."

Look for other Remembered Classics romances
by J L Wilson from The Wild Rose Press, Inc.:
DOGGED
LAKED

Dedication

To VHS Class of 1970
and memories of a simpler, happy time

Chapter 1

The rituals around death give those who are living very little time to immediately grieve. There are forms to fill out, papers to review, music to decide on, a guest list of sorts, relatives to notify. I filled up several sheets of legal paper in the hours after my mother's death, keeping a checklist of things I had to do.

Through a cruel twist of fate, Mom died on Mother's Day Sunday night. I spent most of Monday handling paperwork. Tuesday morning I spent at the funeral home, working out the details. It was the first time I had to plan someone's funeral and the enormity of the task came as a surprise.

My mother had handled all the other deaths in my family. My older brother David died when he was ten in a skating accident. My father died when I was in college and my younger brother Michael died shortly after my father. And my younger brother John died overseas, fighting in an undeclared war no one really cared about or understood.

I thought about my mother often as I prepared for her funeral. She had planned four funerals, three of them for her children. When I was at the drugstore on Tuesday morning, the clerk expressed her sympathy. "Your family sure has had its share of grief," she said with a mournful nod, as though confirming a universal truth. "We all said it was such a shame about the Davis boys. Your mother surely had her share of heartbreak."

I murmured my agreement and my thanks but wondered if anyone thought about the remaining Davis, the Davis girl—me, Wendy? Didn't I have my share of heartbreak, too? I lost brothers, a father, and now my mother. It was as though I was a ghost, a spirit who hovered around those who died. Of course, I hadn't lived in town for a long time so perhaps people had forgotten about me, but I visited often. Didn't that count for something?

Unspoken but there, I knew one other death that clung to me like an extra shadow, a faint echo of times past. Almost thirty years ago, I let someone die and that memory haunted me as surely as if his ghost did.

I walked back from the drugstore to my mom's house, the Davis house, the two-story white frame house on the corner of C Avenue and West Gloucester Street. The May sun was warm on my face and the air smelled of damp earth from last night's rain. Our house was in the "old" part of town where the houses were all two or more stories, the yards were large, and the trees were mature and budding into a fine haze of green overhead.

One house I passed had an entire front flowerbed full of daffodils, the yellow and white flowers bobbing in the breeze. Another house was vibrant with tulips, large masses of varying colors with one special section planted in green and gold, the high school team colors, Pirate colors. I didn't know there were green tulips in the world. I paused to admire the arrangement before continuing my slow walk home.

You can walk just about anywhere in Kensington, Iowa. The town has ten alphabetical and ten numerical north-south avenues, with 1st avenue being the dividing line. There are also eleven east-west streets named for British dynastic houses, crisscrossing at tidy intersections. The town was founded in the mid-1800s and presumably the founding fathers had some nostalgic connection to Britain or maybe just a desire to make tidy, Midwestern streets sound grander than they were.

The old part of town was in the alphabetical avenue section. A suburb of sorts sprang up in recent years on the west side of town, which caused consternation for the city planners because most of the dynastic names were already in use. Consequently, the new streets were named for boroughs of London so we had Greenwich St., Camden Court, Kensington Gardens, and Chelsea Way, keeping with the British Isles theme.

When I was growing up we roamed the streets on our bicycles, ranging from the swimming pool on the east side to the river on the west side. I used to know every house and every alleyway, but change had come to town in the twenty-some years since I went to college then moved away to become a grown-up.

I was at the sidewalk in front of our house, preparing to walk to the front porch, when a car pulled up and the driver leaned across the seat to speak out the open passenger side window. "Wendy? Is that you?"

I didn't recognize the man driving the dark gold Cadillac sedan. He had thinning brown hair, a round face, and a look of pinched worry around his eyes when he peered out at me. "I'm Wendy," I said, going to the passenger window and bending over to look inside. "Who are you?"

"I guess I don't look the way I used to. You look

just about the same, except your hair is short now." He smiled, a crooked smile with one corner of his mouth twisting up. That was what gave him away.

"Dibs?" I asked, leaning into the window to get a good look. "Is it you?"

John Jones, nicknamed Dibs, grinned at me and for an instant I saw the boy from junior high and high school. Back then he was a hyperactive, skinny, beanpole of a kid who aspired to either play professional basketball or become a rock star. He wasn't picky. Either would suffice. His lousy knees and his inability to play guitar halted those dreams. He got his nickname because he was always calling dibs on any fun things we found. The last I knew, he sold cars in Iowa City, forty miles north of Kensington.

"I figured it had to be you," he said. "I heard about your mom. I'm sorry, Wendy." His cheerful grin gave way to an appropriately sober expression. It was odd to see such an adult look on a face I remembered from my youth. Of course, it was odd to see the skinny beanpole change into this rotund man in front of me, too.

"She had a good life, except for these last few months," I said, the oft-repeated words rolling off my tongue and barely registering on my consciousness. "I think she was ready."

I believed that even though Mom died at the relatively young age of seventy-one. That she was ready was what was told to me by the hospice workers and what Mom confirmed for me, if I interpreted her correctly. Mom's massive heart attack and subsequent stroke three months earlier left her almost totally paralyzed except for her eyes, which were amazingly communicative, and her right hand. She and I "talked" a lot at first, but that faltered in the past few weeks when her health began to go downhill at an alarming rate.

"How long are you in town?" Dibs asked.

"At least this week," I said, squatting down near the still-damp grass so I could more easily converse through the open window. "Mom's funeral is on Friday. I'll probably stay through the weekend and into next week, too."

"You're living in Des Moines, right?"

I thought about my two-bedroom condo west of Des Moines in a bustling suburb. "Yes, I am. I'm on a leave of absence from my job right now. Mom was so sick these past few weeks."

"You're a writer or something, aren't you? For some software company?"

I nodded. "I write documentation at Lerner Software. We just wrapped up a big project, so it was okay for me to take some time away. I need to figure out what I'm going to do with the house, take care of the furniture and…" My voice trailed away when I thought of the list of To Do items waiting for me inside. "You know."

"Yeah, I know. My dad died five years ago and I helped Mom with all the stuff. If you need anything, we'd be glad to help. I'm married. You don't know her, I met Barb in college. We have three kids. Anyway, we're glad to help however we can. We live in Iowa City. I'm in town today to see Mom." His cheerful, rambling conversation was exactly as I remembered. Dibs could talk for hours about nothing at all, usually accompanied by elaborate gestures and side stories that left the listener bewildered and lost.

I slowly straightened, my once agile calves protesting slightly. "Thanks, I may take you up on that offer. There's a lot to do."

"I'll try to get to the funeral," he said, his gaze going to the house. "I spent a lot of time here when I was growing up. Seems like we were all here, going in and out."

"Yep. You guys were always underfoot. I think my folks enjoyed it." My father especially loved to have the crowd of boys who always flocked to our house. They were my older brother David's friends and after he died, the boys transferred their friendship to me and my younger brothers. There were always kids playing in our yard or an extra boy or two staying for supper. Our house was the hang-out, the place where everybody congregated.

"Your parents had as much to do with raising us as our own parents did." Dibs started to straighten. "That reminds me. Tom Bell is here."

My heart froze. "Bell? Why?"

Dibs went out of sight when he sat upright again behind the wheel. "I suppose to see you and go to the funeral. He visited your mom a lot these past few years."

I leaned over, almost falling into the expensive leather passenger seat. "He did?"

Dibs frowned, his thick eyebrows drawn together into a solid line. "Yeah. Didn't your mom tell you?"

I tried a nonchalant shrug. "She mentioned he would stop in now and then."

"He and I get together sometimes when he's in town. He lives in New York City now, I think. It seems like he travels a lot. I suppose you knew that, though."

Dibs watched me with frank curiosity, his gray eyes sharp and assessing.

"Yes, I know. He's sure been successful, hasn't he?" My heart was beating so frantically I was certain Dibs would hear it. "Seems like I see his picture in the magazines a lot. I'm surprised the press isn't hounding him."

Dibs laughed. "He told me he has a deal with them. They leave him alone when he's here and he gives 'em a story when he leaves. Everybody in town knows that when he's here, he's just Tommy Bell, Kensington's favorite son. He's not T.K. Bell, former owner of one of the world's biggest computer companies." He shot me a shrewd look. "I read that he's giving up the head office and is going to step into the background. He always said he wanted to retire before he was fifty. Looks like he'll manage it."

I nodded dumbly. Bell was forty-eight, two years older than me. Of all the people I thought I'd see at Mom's funeral, Bell was the one person I didn't expect. "Bell was always a techie," I mumbled. "I'm not surprised he's so successful."

"Your father was, too. I suppose that's why they hit it off so well. Remember that gaming console your dad and Bell built together? That was so cool. Man, we played video games for hours in your basement."

I laughed at the forgotten memory. "Dad later said that building that gaming console probably saved him a thousand dollars or more in the money the kids would have spent at an arcade. And Mom was happy to know where we were—in the basement, playing some game my father and Bell cooked up."

Dibs shot me a shrewd look. "If you still have that

gaming console, I'll bet you could sell it for a bunch of money. It's the first invention that T.K. Bell ever worked on."

He was probably right. It was the first one Bell built, but it certainly wasn't the last one. Bell had made a fortune on innovative hardware and software design, becoming one of the leading figures in computers. He sold his first company, started another one, sold it, started another and was in the process of selling it soon. "I'll look for that console," I said, knowing damn well it had probably been consigned to a recycle bin years earlier. "You're right. Maybe I could make a fortune."

"I wonder what Peter would be doing if he lived."

I backed out of the window, bumping my head on the frame. "Ouch." I rubbed it, my gray-and-black short hair becoming even spikier.

"Peter was the brains of the bunch," Dibs said. "If Bell can end up one of the richest men in the world, Peter probably would have ended up a world leader."

"Or a war criminal," I said sourly. "Peter had a fluctuating sense of morality."

"That's a good way to phrase it." Dibs laughed. "He did, didn't he? Well, I have to go. I'll see you at the funeral on Friday. It was good to see you." He held out a business card and I took it. "Call if you need anything. My mobile number's on there. If I'm not in, just leave a message. I'm glad to help."

"Thanks, Dibs. I appreciate it." I stepped back from the curb and he waved a good-bye before pulling out onto the quiet street.

I looked down at the card with his name in bold letters and a logo of a car dealership imprinted on top of a ghostly image of a Mercedes Benz. *Fine luxury autos for discriminating buyers.* I smiled. Dibs had been one of my favorites among the Lost Boys who hung out at our house. That was the term my mother used for them and it wasn't until I was older and I read *Peter and Wendy* that I realized how appropriate a soubriquet it was. David had been their leader and without him, they were lost.

Until Peter stepped in to lead them. Then they were still lost, but in a different way. I shivered at the memory.

I tucked the card in my jeans pocket and went into the house. By today's modern standards, it was small, with a living room, dining room, and kitchen to the left and a bedroom and bathroom on the right. Upstairs under the eaves were two bedrooms and a tiny bathroom. The boys had one room and I had the other. When their friends stayed overnight, they took over the basement where there was another sleeping area (barely finished and hardly qualifying as a bedroom), a pool table, a roughed-in bathroom, and an old television set on which they played video games all night.

I passed through the living room with the comfortable, casual furniture my mother favored. The couch was brown-and-gold floral with loose cushions and low arms. Two low armchairs in a muted beige plaid were comfortable for curling up with a book in front of her faux fireplace, or to kick back and watch the small TV in the corner.

Athos, Mom's petite mostly-black-with-a-white-tummy cat, looked up from his spot on the back of the sofa, yawned, then settled back to sleep. He was accustomed to me because I was here often. In the past three months, I frequently telecommuted from Mom's house or worked an intensive four-day week so I could have a three-day weekend here. For the past two weeks, I was here most of the time, alternating my time between telecommuting and being with Mom at the hospice where she eventually died.

I went through the dining room with its small round oak table and four chairs, then entered the kitchen, a utilitarian space that was adequate for one person and claustrophobically crowded with two. Mom always joked that Dad made sure we had a small kitchen so he wouldn't have to help, although when we were growing up, somehow it was always crowded with multiple helpers.

I fixed a drink then wandered through the house, unwilling to sit down but with nothing to do. It was an odd, in-between time, two days since Mom died and three days until the funeral. My cousins from Chicago would drive in on Thursday and my cousins from Minneapolis would arrive on Friday. Tomorrow I had to sort through photographs for the video montage the funeral home was setting up. I also needed to work on the eulogy with the minister and iron out a few more details for the service. I might even drive back to Des Moines to swap out some clothes and pick up my mail there. It was only a two-hour drive, but it would be a nice break from my To Do list.

I sipped Mom's bourbon and went into her bedroom, surrounded by the small things that I recognized. I opened the closet and checked the gun safe, hidden under the shoe rack. Dad's Smith & Wesson was still there. He had taught me to shoot when I was a teenager and I still went out to the range now and again using a rental handgun from the range owner.

I meandered back to the living room and sat down, propping my feet up on the overstuffed ottoman and staring out the front window in the living room. Bell was in town. The fact that I pushed to the back of my brain now came into the forefront, demanding attention.

It was hard to believe the press wasn't following him around. He was rich, with homes in the Florida Keys, France, and somewhere in Asia and apartments here and there, wherever his work took him.

It was amazing to think that the boy I dated in high school and college had become such a public figure. He was my first love and I was the one who broke off our relationship. He dropped out of college and traveled the world, taking odd jobs here and there to get by. It was something he always wanted to do, to flit from place to place and see new places and sample the world. It wasn't something I wanted to do and that was one of the reasons we broke up.

When Bell and I dated, it seemed like every time you turned around, somebody was creating a new computer or a new computer game. Bell started programming gaming software, developing several role-playing games long before those became popular. That led to hardware design and that led to a job at Apple which then led to his own company which in turn was sold back to Apple for a hefty profit.

Bell promptly started another company that designed cutting-edge interface technology. He sold that and started yet another company, designing game apps and productivity apps for tablets and smart phones. And now, according to Dibs, he was considering retiring. I used some of Bell's apps daily and I had tried out some the gaming ones. They were clever, easy to use, and engaging. Just like Bell.

The bourbon was warm going down, as warm as the sun shining into the room. It was almost five-thirty. It wouldn't get dark for several hours yet. There was time enough for me to go to the grave. I hadn't visited it in years, but somehow Mom's dying had brought back my youth, making me remember things I successfully pushed to the back of my mind. Things like Bell and Peter and the Lost Boys.

I drained the last of the liquor and set down my glass. I'd go and get it over with. It was a small, niggling thought in the back of my mind, one of those little "I should do that" things that nagged at me. Just do it and be done with it. Don't think about it. I grabbed my purse and my blue sweater then went out the kitchen door to my Jeep mini-SUV in the driveway.

Kensington Gardens, the town cemetery, occupied several acres on the eastern edge of town with a series of roads going through the four quadrants that made up the area. My family was in the southeast quadrant, but Peter was in the northeast side, on a hill overlooking farm fields below. Not far from his grave the bluff fell away, giving a clear view of the land in the distance. He didn't have any family around him. His father had left years before and I think his mother was still alive. She moved away after he died and I lost track of what happened to her.

I pulled onto the grassy edge next to the road and walked to the grave. Fresh flowers were in the small vase attached to the side of the stone. Who did that? I wondered. There wasn't anyone that I knew who would bring flowers to him. But of course, what did I really know about Peter?

I stared down at the gray granite headstone. Just his name and an inscription. No dates to indicate the short length of his life. Nothing to indicate that I was responsible for an eighteen-year-old boy/man taking his own life. Nothing to show that my rejection of him led him to jump out a barn window, which dazed him so badly he stumbled away, jumped in the river, and drowned.

The authorities said it was the alcohol and the drugs. It was one of many graduation parties and Peter drank too much booze, mixing it with pills. He didn't know what he was doing, they said. They made it sound like a tragic accident, which it was, in a way. They didn't understand how unbalanced he really was. They dismissed the argument Peter and I had as just a minor incident.

They didn't know how he wept, how he ran away from me when I told him I didn't love him and when I forced him away from me. They didn't seem to care that he threatened to kill himself if I didn't love him. No one seemed to understand that I pushed him out that window as sure as if I'd shoved him with my hands.

Maybe it was the time lag that kept them from understanding. I was in a car accident the same night and it was a week before the police could talk to me. By then they had tracked Peter from his fall out of the window to the river, where he either threw himself in or fell in. It was weeks before they found his body, washed up thirty miles downstream and identifiable only through dental records.

I was recovering from a broken leg at home. I managed to go to the funeral, with Bell pushing my wheelchair to this sunny and placid hillside. That was in

June and I remember how vibrant the landscape seemed with the fields full of green plants and the farmhouse in the distance, with cows and horses in the pasture. It was so bucolic and serene. It was so opposite that ugly, terrible night when he died.

I wiped away tears and looked down once again at the headstone.

Peter Barry.

Flying among the stars now.

"I thought you'd be here."

I whirled, almost falling over the stone.

It was Bell.

Chapter 2

Years had not changed the face I knew so well from my youth. Oh, there were new lines around his eyes and mouth. And his skin was coarser, not that sweet baby-soft face of his teen years. His dark hair was still long and tousled, falling in soft waves around his square, solid face. It was still sun-streaked although now there was a touch of gray at his temples. His eyes were even more turned down at the corners, making him look sad until he smiled as he always did, with his lips together. Bell never had an open smile except…

Except when we were in bed together. The memory surfaced and vanished like a chill breeze on a warm day.

"Hello, Bell. Dibs said you were in town." I was trembling, caught like some paralyzed animal afraid to move. I don't know what I was afraid of, but there it was.

He nodded. "I saw him the other day." His pale green eyes reflected his sadness. "I was sorry about your mother. She was a special person."

My grief, newly tucked into my memory, swelled afresh. "Thank you," I said, my voice clogged with tears.

He opened his arms and it was the most natural thing for me to go to him. I stumbled and he caught me, holding me tightly against him. I rested my head on his chest, his yellow dress shirt smelling faintly of detergent.

"She was more a mom to me than mine was when we were growing up," he said, his chin resting on my head. Bell was six inches taller than my five-foot-five. That little fact reverberated in my head, mixed up with a bunch of other memories. "I think I spent more time at your house than mine, once I knew your parents wouldn't kick me out."

I leaned back to look up at him and he touched my hair. I kept it short now, shaggy and simple to care for. Unlike him, I was mostly gray and had been since my thirties. I gave up coloring it a long time ago. "Dibs reminded me today how you and my father were such soul mates." I smiled through my tears. "He would have been proud of you, Bell."

"He taught me so much." He ran a finger down the side of my face. "You haven't changed, Wendy. You look just the same except for your hair."

I touched his face, too, gently tracing the white scar near his right eye where an errant baseball almost cost him his sight. "You're the same, too. Except you're famous now."

"I'm not famous here. Here I'm just Tommy Bell, the kid everybody bet would be a juvenile delinquent."

"My parents didn't feel that way." I reluctantly eased away from him, but Bell kept me firmly next to him, his arm around my shoulders. "I think it's because David died so young. I asked Mom about it once and she said it was like she had a big hole in her heart. Having all the kids around helped fill the hole, at least while they were there. She always wanted the house to be full. The more noise, the better."

"That was such a weird accident," Bell said. "Falling down while ice skating and hitting his head. We all did that a million times, didn't we?"

I nodded. "But David got a fractured skull and died." I would never forget that day. I was only eight years old, but I remembered my older brother David's friends coming to the house, Peter and Bell among them. The house was suddenly crowded with people but it was so quiet. It was my first experience with death and its finality.

"We were only ten," Bell said. "Just kids. I'm glad your mother still wanted us around after that. I figured she wouldn't."

"I think she knew you all needed someone. She told me once you were like the Lost Boys from Peter Pan. None of you really had a mother."

Bell smiled, that closed-mouth smile that always made him look sour or sad. "Well, we had mothers, but they weren't like yours."

I smiled, too. My mother had been like a character from *Father Knows Best* or *The Donna Reed Show*. She baked, cooked, cleaned, and generally made our house a home. Bell and Peter's mothers, though, weren't interested in such mundane things. Peter's mother played golf and had cocktails at the country club but scrimped on everything else to afford it. And Bell's mother, well, she just had cocktails and a succession of men who visited her from time to time.

Bell shrugged. "I know that I felt an obligation to David to watch out for you and your brothers. I guess Peter felt the same."

"Who knows what Peter felt?" I asked, trying to keep my voice light.

"Sometimes I don't think even Peter knew." Bell looked down at the grave near our feet.

We were both silent for a long moment, lost in our individual memories. Then I asked, "What brings you back to town?"

"You." He looked down at me. "I wanted to be with you for the funeral." As always, he was simple, direct, and to the point.

"Thank you." I leaned against him, his comforting warmth an antidote to the sudden chill that made me shiver. "Where are you staying?"

He laughed softly. "Didn't you know? I'm a major stakeholder in that new motel they built out by the hospital. I had a suite built there for me."

The "new" two-story Kensington Arms Motel was built ten years before on the west side of town, just six blocks away from Mom's house. It was a significant improvement over the old ten-room roadside motel that had served travelers for half a century. "I'm sure it's not the Ritz or the Savoy," I said, moving away from him. A suite at the Kensington was probably two cramped rooms with a whirlpool tub in the john.

His eyes narrowed at my jibe. "It's clean, quiet, and private. That's all I really need."

"Not according to the magazine stories I've read about you." I walked past Peter's grave to the edge of the bluff. An oak tree, probably a hundred years old, towered over me. It was just losing its leaves to new spring growth and the lawn underneath was strewn with brown detritus. "You're a celebrity, Bell. It seems like you flit from hot spot to hot spot, always with the most beautiful people. You're the most eligible bachelor in the world."

He joined me on the bluff. "Don't believe everything you read."

I regarded him skeptically. "Oh, you're not a bachelor? One of those movie stars finally snagged you? I've seen pictures of you with some gorgeous women."

Bell dug his hands into his jeans pockets and scuffed at the leaves with one sneakered toe. "Yeah, well, it makes for good publicity. It doesn't mean anything. What about you? You were married, weren't you?"

"Briefly." I wrinkled my nose at the memory. "I'd rather be single than married to someone who's perpetually jealous. The way he acted, I was a femme fatale, breaking men's hearts from here to the stars and back again."

"To the stars and back again," Bell repeated softly. "I haven't heard that for a long time."

That had been our catch phrase back when we were growing up. *I'll race you to the stars and back again. I caught holy hell to the stars and back again.* I looked over my shoulder at the grave, set slightly apart from the others. "It'll be thirty years in a few weeks. I can't believe it. I remember it like it was yesterday. Parts of it, at least."

"You still blame yourself, don't you?" Bell wasn't looking at me. He was staring into the distance at the farm and the animals milling around in the pasture.

"I do, but I'm still confused by it all. It's the only explanation that makes sense. I can't imagine that Peter would kill himself unless—" I didn't finish. I didn't have to. Bell was there that night. He heard it all.

"What do you mean, you're confused?"

"I had no idea Peter felt that way about me. You and I were a couple and the only reason I went with Peter that night was because you and I had that stupid fight." I followed Bell's gaze to the farm, noticing several cars in the drive. The family there must be having a reunion. "Peter didn't have time to fall in love with me. He and I were always just friends. Why did he decide all of a sudden that he couldn't live without me?"

Bell nodded. "That never made sense to me, either. Another thing that never made sense was our car accident."

"What?" This was something that I had never considered. When Peter ran away from me that night, throwing himself out the barn window, I ran after him. Bell was downstairs and after a semi-coherent explanation of what happened, he and I took Bell's old Impala and went after Peter. The party where this all happened was west of town near the river, on a farm owned by Jamie Lim, the hippie guidance counselor at the school.

Bell and I drove down the farm lane and got as far as the main road when a front tire exploded. Bell couldn't control it and we caromed into the ditch. We were thrown out because seat belts weren't common then. Bell suffered a broken arm and multiple contusions. I got a broken leg. When I emerged from a drugged fog at the hospital, Peter was dead, drowned in the river.

"What do you mean the car accident didn't make sense?" I faced Bell, who still stared at the farm over my right shoulder.

He pulled me to him, his hands on my shoulders so

he could look into my face. "I think we need to talk somewhere more private."

I looked around. "It's a cemetery. It doesn't get much more private than this."

He looked over my shoulder. "There are photographers down there, probably equipped with telephoto lenses. Your picture is going to be in the tabloids tomorrow."

I turned to see but he kept me in place with his hands. "I thought you had a deal with them," I protested. "That's what Dibs said."

"The deal was they couldn't come into town." He nodded toward the farm. "That's not town. I'm sorry, Wendy. It looks like you're going to become a celebrity."

"Well, crapola," I muttered. "I'm nobody famous. Why do they care about me?"

Bell lowered his head and our lips met in a gentle kiss. "That's why," he whispered. "Because you're the woman in my life."

"What?" I sputtered, once again trying to pull away from his firm grasp of my shoulders. "I am not. I was the woman, once, but I'm not anymore."

"As far as they're concerned, you're my mystery woman." He put an arm around my shoulders and we started back to Peter's grave. "Let me handle it. They may come into town now. This is a big story for them."

"Bell, this is ridiculous." I let him lead me to my car. A red-brown Ford Explorer was parked behind my smaller Jeep Compass. "There is no story."

"They'll find one. Let's go to your house and drop off your car then go to the hotel. I want to talk about what happened that night. I've done some digging and I think maybe things aren't what they seemed."

I paused, my hand on my door handle. "What?"

"Let's talk." He went to his car, leaving me gaping at him.

I drove to Mom's house, my brain whirling. The first shocker was that Bell was here, in town. I was surprised how relieved I was that he was here. I was dreading Mom's funeral because of the endless line of mourners that I knew would attend. She had lived in Kensington all her life and been active in the community, serving on a million different volunteer committees. The refrigerator at the house, stuffed with food that people dropped off, told me how loved she was. Having Bell with me would make everything easier.

How odd that we reconnected like this after so many years. I last saw him about ten years earlier. He was in town and I was visiting my mother. Bell came to the house for supper and it was eerily like old times and yet it wasn't. Instead of the big rectangular six-person table, we now had a small four-person round table. The ghosts of my father and my brothers seemed to hover around us while we talked and laughed. I can't count the number of times that dining room was full to overflowing with Lost Boys milling around and eating Mom's famous homemade pizza.

I pulled into the driveway at the house and parked my car, waiting for Bell to get out of his where he pulled up behind me. Instead he gestured me to him. "Get in," he said when I neared.

"Where are we going?"

"You'll see."

I frowned skeptically at him but climbed into the

SUV and buckled up. "Won't the photographers see your car at the motel?" I asked while he drove west on Gloucester Street.

"I've got that covered. When they built it, I had them build a special section for me." He glanced at me and grinned mischievously. "What's the point of being the owner of a motel if you can't make a few modifications?"

"Owner? You said you were a shareholder."

"I under-exaggerated."

I laughed. "That's not an expression."

"Sure it is. I just made it up."

I ran my hand over the dark brown leather seat. This was obviously a luxury edition given the leather trim on the dash, the plush seats, and the gadgetry displayed in the in-dash screen. "Nice car. Did you rent it?"

"Nope. I leave it here." He drove by St. Jude's hospital, moving to one side to let an ambulance scream past us. "I like having wheels when I'm in town and the closest rental is Iowa City."

I nodded, not really tracking what he said. As we turned into the parking lot for the hotel, his words registered. "Well, how do you get from the airport in Iowa City to here, then?"

"I don't fly into Iowa City. I have a plane. I fly in to the airport outside of town."

"You own a plane?"

"Just a small one. Four passenger."

"You fly it here? What airport? I thought the airport was just a concrete strip in the middle of a cornfield."

"It's big enough for a Cessna. Here we are." Bell

pressed a button above the windshield.

"We're where?" He had the car idling in front of the rear door of the motel. The building was modular-appearing, with four windows per side per module, two up and two down. There were five modules, which I assumed meant forty rooms, eight per module. Bell was idling in front of the last four windows which—

Holy crapola. The lower two windows were a facade. The one at the end of the building lifted up and back, revealing a one-car garage. Bell pulled the SUV forward and closed the door behind us. He smiled at my open-mouthed astonishment. "I like my privacy. This whole section is mine." He shut off the SUV and hopped out.

I followed, still stunned. I knew that Bell was wealthy, but it hadn't really soaked in. Now I found out he had a luxury SUV that he kept here for a trip now and then, he had a plane, he owned a hotel specialized just for him, and—and Lord knows what else. I trailed behind him while we went through a door leading to an open area with stairs going up and a large TV, couches, and a pool table set against the far wall.

At the top of the steps we came into what should have been four motel rooms. What I saw instead was a living room and a kitchen with an island that served as a dining space, all open and beautifully decorated with simple Mission-style furniture. On the far wall was a short hallway with two doors opening off it.

"That's regular bedrooms," Bell said, gesturing to the hallway. "I took the other two rooms and made them living space. Have a seat. Do you want a drink? How about something to eat? I've got some cold chicken and pea salad." He strode to the small kitchen.

"It's made according to your mom's recipe, so you know it's good."

"I can't believe you did all this." I followed him to the kitchen and took a seat at the large square island separating one space from another. "And you kept it all a secret."

"I like coming back here to visit." Bell opened the fridge and pulled out tonic water then opened the freezer and pulled out gin. "I wanted someplace to stay when I come and the town needed a good motel. It made sense." He got insulated tumblers out of a cupboard and began mixing drinks at the counter next to the fridge.

He said it so casually, I knew that it wasn't odd to him. Bell saw a need for the town and a need for himself, and he did the most efficient thing he could do to fill both needs. I guess the only real question I had was why he continued to visit Kensington, Iowa when he had homes in such exotic spots as the Keys or L.A. I knew if I asked him he'd tell me, but I wasn't sure I wanted to hear the answer. Not yet, anyway.

"How's your mom doing? I lost track of her after she moved away." His mother left town when Bell graduated from high school. Her leaving had gone almost unnoticed in the turmoil after Peter's death.

"She bounced around from here to there then ended up in Vegas with husband number four. She died about five years ago from cancer."

I started to say *I'm sorry,* but Bell and his mother had a problematic relationship because she spent most of his adolescence in an alcoholic haze, letting him raise himself. "I'll bet she was proud of you. You've become such a success."

"I think it surprised her. She was happy to have me support her and her husband. He was a down-on-his-luck gambler. I kept him supplied with enough money to keep them both happy." Bell had his back to me so I couldn't see his face, but I heard the bitterness he hid under his light-hearted tone of voice. "The last I heard he was on wife number six and she was bankrolling him." He turned and handed me a frosty glass. "Cheers."

"Thanks." I sipped, watching him while he set out a cold roast chicken from the grocery store and a Tupperware container of salad. He looked the same as I remembered, with a slender, lean build. Bell was the runner who excelled at track and field. Peter was the football player, a running back with the high school's Kensington Pirates. He was fast but not in the same league as Bell. "You haven't changed, Bell."

"I'm just a bit creased, that's all." He came around the counter and sat next to me at the kitchen island on a tall chair. "You don't look like you've aged except for your hair. It's like your mother's. Her hair was always gray, too."

"Hers turned gray when David died," I said, taking one of the plates he set out and helping myself to chicken. "I think I take after Dad."

"Your father really did teach me a lot. I owe him and your family." He sliced off a bit of chicken and put it on his plate along with a healthy dollop of pea salad, the yummy concoction my mother always made for him.

I tried a sample of it and nodded appreciatively. "I think you've nailed it, Bell. It tastes just like Mom's."

He looked pleased. "I asked her for the recipe one

time when I came over to visit. I got it and a bunch of other ones, including the pizza crust recipe."

I stared at him in mock surprise. "She didn't share her secret crust recipe, did she?"

"She did. I'll make you pizza tomorrow if you'd like. What are you doing? Are you busy?"

"I have to go through photos and take some to the funeral home. They want to put together one of those photo montages to play during the service." I thought of the photo albums stored in the upstairs closet and sighed. "I need to go visit Aunt Jane, too, and make sure to keep her in the loop about what's going on. And I haven't inventoried the safety deposit box yet. I need to get that done, too."

"I forgot about Aunt Jane. Where is she?"

"She has an assisted living apartment, attached to St. Jude's. She's still pretty spry for somebody who's seventy-seven with arthritis. Almost everything else is finalized. The cousins start to arrive on Thursday."

"It'll be standing room only at her service."

"I know. I'm dreading it."

Bell covered my left hand with his right hand. He had long, blunt fingers, strong and capable. "I'll be there with you if you'll let me."

I leaned against him. "Thank you."

"I wasn't kidding, you know. The press will be hounding you. They'll want to know if you and I are a hot item."

I looked up at him. Our faces were just inches apart. "I'm not in the same league as those women I see you with in the tabloid."

"No, you aren't." He leaned closer. "You're to the stars and back again better."

Chapter 3

I started to lean forward then I stopped. "I'm not going to fall in love with you again."

He stopped, too. "Why not?"

I hopped off the swivel bar seat. "Because I live in Des Moines and you live everywhere else. Because you're rich and famous. Because I'm forty-six years old and happy to be an old maid. I don't want to be a celebrity."

"You're hardly a maid," Bell said with a mischievous grin. "I don't know what kind of love life you had with your husband, but I do remember our love life, and you're no maid, Wendy Darling." He used my old nickname tenderly, just the way I remembered.

My face got hot and I went to the fridge, jerking open the door and peering inside so he wouldn't see me. I pulled out a jar of pickles and turned to put them on the kitchen island. The mundane action helped me cool off and when I looked at him, I could hold his gaze without flinching. "I haven't seen you in more than twenty years. A lot can happen in twenty years. I've changed and you have, too."

"How do you know?" His green eyes were mischievous, just as I remembered him when he would challenge me to an argument, knowing damn well he had an ace up his sleeve that would assure him of a victory.

Well, it wasn't going to work this time. "I know I've changed. I'm happy with the life I have."

"Really? Making eighty-thousand a year and writing documentation for a product that probably should have gone into maintenance mode a long time ago. That can't be that fulfilling."

I glared at him, outraged. "You checked up on me."

"Yep. Your mother was worried about you. She said you seemed bored with your job and your life. Three weeks of vacation a year and most of that spent in visits to family or friends or going to the Ozarks."

"There's nothing wrong with the Ozarks," I protested. "Besides, it's none of your business how I spend my free time. I haven't seen you for decades, and you show up and act like you want to pick up where we left off. It's not that simple, Bell. For heaven's sake, you're a bazillionaire. You probably have designer houses and designer suits and designer parties that you go to. I'm not going to get tangled up in that."

Bell watched me, his face thoughtful. "Are you really worried about all the success crap? I never thought you'd be insecure about something like that."

His words stung but I wasn't going to let him know. "I don't think I'm insecure. It's more like common sense. Let's face it, Bell. I'm not the girl I used to be. You can have your pick of anybody. This is all just some nostalgic jag you're on. You loved Mom, too, and you're trying to hold on to the past or something."

He looked down at his plate then up at me through his long dark eyelashes. "I understand why you feel that way. And you might be right, at least a little bit. There's one thing I want you to consider, though. What if you're wrong? What if I tell you I'm retiring and I can live wherever I want and do whatever I want? And what I want is to find a quiet spot to settle down, build a nice house customized the way I want it, and fiddle around with my apps. Within two weeks the press will forget all about me except for once a year or so when they have a 'Whatever happened to' issue and somebody tracks us down."

"I don't love you." I said it with as much conviction as I could muster. I almost convinced myself. "Not that way, at least. You're someone from my past who I used to love, and I do love the connection you have with my family. Now that I'm alone, I admit it. It's nice to have someone here to share Mom's funeral and to have someone to help me. But I don't love you."

"Yes, you do. You're just afraid to admit it." He stated it as a fact, like saying *look, the sun's shining* or *I have a plane and I land at the airport here in town.*

"You always were an over-confident, arrogant s.o.b.," I snapped.

"And you were always hesitant unless you were pushed. And I was usually the one doing the pushing." He smiled then, deep dimples punctuating his cheeks. "Think about it, Wendy. We could have some fun. That's all I'm asking. We have a lot of shared history together. Let's at least see if we don't have the chance for a shared future."

I started to snap a sharp retort but his warm, laughing eyes made me hesitate. He was right, damn it. I was always the cautious one, the one who hung back and peered over the edge before jumping. Bell was the one who never looked before he leaped, although he almost always landed on his feet. If he didn't, I was there to pick up the pieces, just like he picked up the pieces for me.

"I'll consider it, Bell. That's all I'll say for now." I sought a topic to divert his attention from me. "What kinds of apps are you going to do? More reality apps? Or are you going to branch off into more games?"

"Reality apps are going strong right now. Have you tried Wendy Darling's Day?" he asked. "It's a huge seller. All the retro stuff is very fashionable right now."

WDD was one of his 'reality' apps, which allowed users to set up profiles, create characters, and act out different scenarios. Wendy Darling was a teenage girl whose avatar looked suspiciously like me when I was in high school, complete with long brown hair in a tumbling, Farah Fawcett style. She could get into all kinds of scrapes, depending on what the users of the app made her do.

"I should get royalties for that," I pointed out. "You modeled it after everything I did in high school. Who the heck buys that app?"

"Teenage girls and their mothers. They love it. Mothers have written me and told me how it's brought them so much closer to their girls." He regarded me thoughtfully. "You know, you're right. You should get royalties. I'll talk to my legal team about that."

"I was kidding, Bell."

"I'm not." He pulled out a smart phone and tapped something on it. "I'll give them a call tomorrow. They're East Coast time, so they're out of the office now."

"I was kidding." I reached for his phone but he

tucked it back in his shirt pocket before I could grab it.

"Let's talk about Peter instead of your royalties."

His words stopped my racing brain in its tracks. "What about Peter?"

"Let's sit in the living room. Get comfortable." Bell came around the kitchen island and helped me put away the food then he picked up our drinks and led the way to a beautiful Mission style couch upholstered in dark green fabric. Two half-round oak end tables with inlaid wood designs flanked it.

Bell set his glass on one end table and handed me my drink before he sat. Two matching chairs faced us with a burnished oak coffee table with the same inlaid design between us. A large picture of a lake with a boat in the distance hung on the opposite wall.

"I always wondered what happened afterward." Bell regarded me steadily. "It was like Peter died and life just went on."

I sipped my drink then set the glass on the coffee table, centering it on a cloth coaster that was a replica of one of Frank Lloyd Wright's famous prairie-style stained glass windows. "What do you mean? You graduated from high school and went to college. I spent most of the summer recovering from a broken leg. I had one more year of high school then I graduated and went to college." I had skipped a grade in elementary school, so although I was two years younger than Bell, I was only one year behind him in school. "Then my father got sick and you and I broke up and life got really busy. I was trying to be a grown-up and got my first real job and first apartment."

"We should never have broken up." Bell said it almost belligerently, like an accusation. "You and I always got along so good together."

"Of course we had to break up. You were itching to travel around the world and see what there was to see. I wanted to stay home. It would never have worked. I was always a home-and-hearth kind of person, and you were always a go-out-and-explore kind of person."

"We complemented each other. You kept me grounded and I gave you wings."

I rolled my eyes. "You're looking at this through a fog of memory." I decided to ignore his supposed fascination with me and returned to the subject at hand. "What did you mean about what happened afterward? You were around. You know."

"Not really. I was in college. What happened to Jamie Lim?" Bell asked. He put his arm along the back of the couch, almost touching me.

"Lim? The guidance counselor?" I shivered, remembering the suave, hip young counselor who tried so hard to blend in with the students. He was just a few years older than us, in his twenties when he worked at our high school. He often had parties at the farm he and his friend Johnny Smead rented. Smead worked in Iowa City as a bartender and was a wine connoisseur, or so he said. "I never liked him. He had too much hair."

Bell laughed. "Said the woman who had more hair than a supermodel back then." He ruffled my short, shaggy hair. "I like this better, I think, although I have to admit, you had a nice head of hair back then. Anyway, what happened to Lim and Smead?"

I tried to remember my senior year in high school. Bell and I were dating and I spent a lot of time in Iowa City, where Bell was a college student living off-campus in a tiny studio apartment not much bigger than a closet. "I think he was gone during my senior year."

Bell nodded. "Once I had real money, I started doing some checking. I hired detectives to go back and dig through records. Lim was fired after that party where Peter was hurt. The school hushed it up and the police cooperated with the school. Nobody wanted a scandal. Imagine what would happen today if that happened—kids attending a party at an adult's house, someone who works for the school, and drugs and alcohol being served. Lim would probably have ended up in prison. But the school officials covered it up."

He took a sip of his drink then continued. "Lim and Smead were gone before they even found Peter's body ten days later. It took a lot of digging, but I found out they went to Laguna Beach, where they lived on Smead's salary. I don't think Lim ever worked again. Like I said, he's lucky he wasn't prosecuted. They were gay, you know."

He tossed that out like a casual bombshell. I nodded slowly. At the time, "gay" wasn't something that people talked about. When you're a kid, people keep things from you, and it's only when you're an adult and look back that you realize what was really going on. "I suppose you're right," I said. "I guess I never thought about it."

"Peter was bisexual."

I stared at Bell, open-mouthed. "He had a girlfriend," I reminded him. "That's one reason I was so surprised when he told me how much he loved me. He and Tina had gone together for almost a year." I frowned. "Whatever happened to her?"

"My detectives found her, too. Tina Lilly died not long after graduation. She went to California.

Coincidentally, she lived not far from Peter's mother, who moved there after Peter died. Tina drowned in the ocean a few months after she moved there."

"Really? Wow." I didn't like Tina, who was an arrogant, statuesque girl who acted like she owned Peter. "But wait a minute. You said he was bisexual. How do you know?" He leveled a gaze at me that made my face get hot again. "Holy crapola, did he come on to you?"

Bell nodded. "Peter was really ambivalent about his sexuality. I think Lim seduced him at least once. You know Peter's father was gay?"

I shook my head. "How do you know that?" Peter's parents were only eighteen years older than us. They married young and his mother had Peter when she was just a teen.

"Those detectives I hired. They found what happened to Peter's father. Remember when his father and mother got divorced? It was when Peter was ten or so. His father left and I had the detectives track him down. He lived with another man in Berkley."

"Holy crapola," I muttered, my brain spinning. "Is that why Peter tried to rape me? Was he trying to prove his manhood or something?"

"What?" Bell sat up straighter. "You never told me that."

"Maybe rape is too strong. He wouldn't take no for an answer. I had to hit him to get him to stop. That's when he got off me and we argued."

"You never told me that. You told me your shirt got torn when you fell down the steps."

"I lied. I was afraid you'd beat Peter to a pulp if I told you."

35

Bell flexed his fingers. "I would have."

"Then it's a good thing I never told you, isn't it?" I considered what he said. "Why do you care about Jamie Lim?"

"I just think it's odd that the party happened at his house and he left so soon afterward, that's all." Bell propped his right ankle on his left knee and jiggled it, deep in thought. "Did your mother leave you anything?"

The change of subject caught me by surprise, making me take a bigger swallow of gin than I planned. I almost choked when liquor went down the wrong pipe. "What do you mean?" I managed to gasp.

"She told me once that she had information about that night."

"How often did you visit her?" I eyed him suspiciously.

He avoided my gaze, twisting on the couch to reach for his drink on the end table. "Now and then. Did she leave you anything?"

"I haven't gone through the safety deposit box yet. Maybe there's something there."

"OK. Let's go there tomorrow."

"I didn't invite you."

He stuck out his lower lip. "Really?"

"Oh, okay." Truth be told, I would be happy for his company. The constant outpouring of sympathy was beginning to wear on my nerves. Having him along would be a buffer between me and the people at the bank where Mom and Dad had their accounts for so many years. "I get the feeling you have an idea about what you want to find. Care to clue me in?"

"Peter's parents took out a half-million-dollar

insurance policy on him when he was just a kid. When they got divorced, it was part of the divorce agreement that his father continue to make the payments. Sylvia was the beneficiary."

"What's that got to do with my mom's safe deposit box? And besides, Peter committed suicide," I protested. "Life insurance won't pay out on suicide."

"It wasn't suicide." Bell sipped his drink. "It's listed as 'cause of death unknown.' "

I always assumed it was investigated as a suicide. But now that I thought about it, I guess I never read anything official about it. My parents were with me when I struggled back to consciousness and they said that Peter died. No one talked about it except for whispered mutterings in the hallway of the hospital.

By the time I finished physical therapy for my broken leg and went back to school in the fall, the usual resiliency of youth had asserted itself and we all moved on. "Don't tell me. Your detectives dug up the cause of death."

"Actually, they dug up that there is no listed cause of death." Bell looked down at his glass. "It's a matter of public record. I just think it's odd that everyone associated with his death left town."

"Lim was probably fired. You went to college. The other kids at the party were graduating and most of them left town. So?" I shrugged. "That's what happens after graduation. People leave."

"I was thinking more about the grown-ups. Sylvia left town the winter after Peter went missing."

"Went missing? He was buried, Bell. She identified his body."

"She didn't identify anything. The body was

identified by the dental records."

"Well, see. That proves it was Peter." I sipped my drink, wondering what he was getting at. In the years following Peter's death, I had managed to shove my guilt about Peter's behavior onto the back burner of my brain. All this talk with Bell heated up those memories and I was more than a little resentful about it.

"It doesn't prove anything. Did you know that Sylvia worked as a volunteer at the Vietnam Vets Outreach Center in Iowa City?"

That surprised me. Sylvia Barry was a self-centered wannabe socialite. It was hard to image her volunteering to help homeless vets. "She volunteered. What does that mean?"

"Peter had his dental work done there. His father was a vet, so Peter had privileges there. His mother couldn't afford orthodontia and he had to use the free clinic to have basic work done. She scrimped on everything just so she could join the country club and act richer than she was. How many nights did Peter come to your house for supper?"

I started to deny it then a small memory nudged me. "Dreams and stardust," I muttered.

"What?"

"My mother used to say that Peter's mother lived on dreams and stardust, but it was silly to expect a growing boy to live on them, too. My mother didn't have a lot of patience with Sylvia Barry."

Bell smiled. "I can imagine your mother saying that. She was practical. But she had a dreams and stardust side, too."

"What do you mean?"

"Sometimes when I visited we would go for long

drives. She would roll down the car window and let the breeze blow through the car. I gave her some CDs and she brought them with her and she'd sing along."

My mother? Listening to CDs and singing along? I could imagine it but it was hard.

"She liked to go out to the lake. We'd go for a walk near the shelter there and she would take bread to toss to the birds. I think she had the knack for attracting the pelicans. They would wait politely for her, not jostling each other, and she would toss out bread to each one individually."

My mother never mentioned pelican tossing to me. Of course, she never mentioned Bell's visits either, so why was I surprised?

"She called them the Never birds. She said they were so odd looking, they shouldn't be in Iowa, in the middle of farmland." Bell pursed his lips thoughtfully. "They are exotic, aren't they? I think that's what she meant. She had her dreams and stardust side."

I took a long swallow of watered-down gin, trying to cool a faint simmer of jealousy. I made a mental note to check that box of music tapes and CDs of Mom's that I had set to one side. I hadn't even glanced at the titles while I was packing her belongings but now I wondered what music Bell brought for her. She obviously listened to it enough to sing along with it.

I jerked my mind from the subject of Bell and my mother. "I still don't see why it matters that Peter had his dental work done at the free clinic."

Bell sighed. "You used to be smarter than this."

I glared at him. "Maybe if I knew what you were leading up to, I might be able to add two and two."

Bell ticked off points on his fingers. "There was a

fat life insurance policy on Peter. His mother worked at the place where his dental records were stored. She left town not long after his death. She invested the money she got from the insurance policy and she's now relatively wealthy."

"Relatively?" I muttered. "Is that compared to you?"

"Don't be snide. Think, Wendy. What does it mean?"

"You're saying Sylvia killed Peter so she could get the insurance money?" I shook my head, denying it even as I said it. "Peter jumped out that window. He went to the river and threw himself in. It's only dumb luck and charity on the part of the authorities it wasn't listed as suicide. There's nothing to prove that Sylvia killed him."

"That's not what I'm saying." Bell looked down at his glass, rattling the ice cubes. "I'm saying Peter is still alive. They faked it all."

Chapter 4

I almost dropped my gin glass. "That's crazy."

"Is it?"

"Why would Peter fake his own death?" This made no sense.

"Think about it. Think about what half-a-million dollars meant back then."

I started to protest but the words died before I could speak them. He was right. That kind of money wasn't chump change, no matter when you're talking about. And years ago, it was a boatload of cash. Maybe there was motivation after all.

"Is he with her? With Sylvia? How did they— why—where are they—what—" I was stammering, trying to articulate my shock. I had gone from incredulity to tentative acceptance in the blink of an eye. All these years I thought Peter was lying in a grave and now Bell says—"Wait a minute. Who's in the grave?"

Bell shot me a disbelieving look. "Sylvia worked with homeless vets. You figure it out."

"But—you mean she murdered someone and substituted his dental records for Peter's? That's insane. Sylvia didn't have the kind of smarts to pull that off. Heck, Sylvia didn't have the guts to pull off something like that."

"But Peter did."

Any further protest was totally squashed. He was right. Peter was brainy and clever and ruthlessly cold when he wanted to be. If anyone could figure out how to fake his own death, it would be Peter. Suddenly my bemusement changed to outrage. "That asshole," I muttered. "All these years I've been blaming myself because I thought I was the cause of Peter's death."

"I hate to say it, but if I'm right, you were a convenient excuse and that's all."

I glared at him. "Thanks."

"A beautiful, naïve, convenient excuse," he amended. "If it's any consolation, he made us all feel that way. You, me, Jamie Lim, the authorities—poor Peter, depressed and alone." Bell smiled wryly. "You're in good company. And to answer your other question, the detectives have taken pictures of Sylvia with a younger man, but he doesn't look anything like Peter."

"Maybe it's a Boy Toy," I muttered. "Sylvia always did have an eye for the guys."

Bell shook his head. "No, it doesn't look like that. They're friends, but not that friendly. He's the right height and build for Peter, and the hair color is similar, but the face is all wrong."

"Plastic surgery?" I ventured. Then I heard what I said. "Holy crapola, I can't believe I'm buying into this. It's crazy to even think it."

"Why? If you can imagine it, why isn't it possible? If I'm right," Bell said with heavy emphasis, "Peter and Sylvia are living the good life in California."

I thought about it for a minute. "What can we do about it? How do you prove that they defrauded the insurance company?"

"I'm not sure. I have some ideas."

"What would happen? Sylvia is in her sixties now. Would she go to prison?"

"I suppose so. I don't know. I do know that I don't think it's right that they get away with it." Bell looked down at his glass. "There's something else. I was with your mom the day before she had her stroke," he said quietly. "I've worried that maybe something I said caused it. She and I went out for a ride. She had been going through some of your father's things. She asked me if I wanted his journals."

Dad kept notebooks of ideas for years. We called them his Inspiration Spirals. "I didn't know she still had them."

He nodded. "She said she kept them and had been looking through a couple of them. She seemed puzzled by something in his journal. She asked me a lot of questions about what happened the night Peter jumped out that window."

"Really? Mom and I hadn't talked about it in years. Why would she bring it up?"

"I'm not sure. When I told her what I remembered, she seemed upset. I was afraid that maybe I said something that disturbed her."

"Of course not," I said, answering his unspoken worry instead of the actual facts. "What could you do or say that would cause a stroke?"

He shook his head. "I don't know. The first I knew she was sick was when I called her house a few days later and somebody else answered."

"What? Who answered?"

"Your Aunt Jane. She told me what happened. I think she was at the house getting some things for your mom in the hospital."

I nodded. That made sense.

"You know somebody visited your mom the day she had her stroke?"

"Who visited her?"

"Your aunt wasn't sure. She called your mother and your mother just said that she had company."

"What do you mean she called Mom?"

Bell sighed patiently. "I visited your mom. Then the next day somebody else visited her. Your aunt called while the visitor was there and your mom said someone was there. She said it was an old friend. Your aunt assumed it was me and it wasn't until later that we compared notes and I realized that someone else visited her." He looked expectantly at me, as though I had the answer to this mystery guest.

"Since I didn't even know that you were visiting her or how often you were visiting her, I have no idea who it might have been." I eyed Bell accusingly, but he ignored my look.

"I wonder if that visitor had anything to do with her stroke."

It took a second for the meaning to soak in. "What?"

"It's odd that she was asking me about the day Peter vanished, then a day or two later, she has a catastrophic stroke and she loses most of her memory and her ability to speak. Your mother was in good health and she was young to have a stroke like that."

I shook my head. "You sound paranoid."

"Just because I'm paranoid, that doesn't mean somebody isn't behind it all."

"There's no way to prove anything." I touched his hand. "Mom had a stroke, Bell. It happens. She had arterial disease and the doctor said it might happen."

"I know. Maybe I am grasping at straws, trying to find a reason where there isn't anything there." Bell drained the last of his gin in one belligerent swallow. "It's just that—if Sylvia and Peter got away with faking his death, they should be brought to justice but I don't know if it'll happen."

"Why do you care?" I shrugged when he glared at me. "They're not hurting anyone, are they? Okay, okay, they're criminals, but—"

"Criminal? That's a mild word for somebody who faked his death, either killed someone or caused someone to die and then got off free with thousands of dollars. They defrauded everyone."

"Us included?" I prompted.

Bell didn't reply immediately and I waited. I knew from past experience that when he was ready to talk about an uncomfortable subject, he would, and not a moment earlier. "Yes, I am pissed off that they fooled us," he finally said. "I wondered for years if my argument with Peter was what triggered his actions."

"Your argument? I thought my argument caused him to jump. What argument did you have with him?"

Bell sighed. "I haven't told you everything that happened that night."

"Well, maybe it's time you did." When he didn't speak, I added, "That's not a request, Bell. It's a demand."

He sighed again. "After you and I argued and we broke up, Peter approached me at school. It was the afternoon of the party."

"What did we argue about?" I asked. "I don't remember."

45

He shrugged. "Whatever it was, you were pissed off enough to break up with me."

I stared at him incredulously. "You broke up with me."

Bell shook his head. "Nope. You broke up with me." When I started to protest, he hurried on. "No matter who broke up with who, the bottom line was we decided to split up. We had planned to go to that party together, but when Peter found out we weren't a couple any more, he told me that he was going to take you. I got mad and took a swing at him."

"What?" This was the first I heard that Bell and Peter weren't the best of friends right up until the moment Peter died—or supposedly died.

"It was after baseball practice. Peter told me that he had always wanted to go out with you and now that you were free, he was going to ask you out. I took a swing at him. Curly and Dibs broke up the fight." Bell rattled the ice cubes in his empty glass. "That's why I came looking for you at the party. I decided that no matter what happened, I didn't want to break up with you. It didn't matter who was right or wrong. You and I belonged together."

"I went to the party with Mary and some other girls." It was amazing how clear the memory of that party was, even after all these years. Of course, it was a life-changing event for almost everybody involved, so I suppose that was why. "Peter told me that you were up in the loft and you wanted to see me. I was so happy we weren't mad at each other anymore, I believed everything he said. He and I went up into the loft and that's when he attacked me." Jamie Lim's old barn was the hangout for kids who liked to smoke dope, listen to risqué music, and make out, usually up in the hay loft. Bell and I never made out there. We had a private spot we liked out south of town. Bell's car was big enough to make it fun.

"I was so pissed off. Curly told me that Peter told him he was taking you out. The way Curly talked, it sounded like an orgy or something. That's when I showed up at the farm."

"I pushed Peter away and he ran straight for the loft window and jumped." The big window was more of a doorway with a rope and pulley. Farmers could pull hay wagons in underneath and lift the bales up into the loft. I scrambled down out of the loft after Peter jumped and literally fell into Bell's arms.

"That was a twenty- or thirty-foot drop," Bell said. "I still don't know how he didn't break an ankle. But he didn't. He ran through the field to the river." He squinted, probably visualizing the scene. "We should go out to the farm and look around."

"It's been decades. The barn is probably torn down by now." I tried to remember what happened to the farm, but if my mother had mentioned it to me, I'd long forgotten any details. "Maybe we should each try to write down what we remember about that night then compare notes." I looked at the clock on the wall in the kitchen, surprised to see it was almost seven. "I need to get home. I still have those photographs to go through tonight."

"I can help," Bell volunteered.

"No, it's something I need to do on my own," I said firmly. "I appreciate the offer, though."

"I'd like to help with something." He took my hand. "Your mom was a big part of my life. I couldn't be here when your father died, so I'd like to do something now."

Bell had been off on his world travels when Dad got cancer of the jaw and died. His death was mercifully swift and Mom did get a long sympathy letter from Bell, months after the fact. It had pissed me off at the time that he didn't try to get home. Bell was like a son to my father and I know Dad wanted to see him before he died.

Well, that was years in the past. There was no use carrying a grudge. I got to my feet and went to the kitchen, setting my glass in the sink. "You can go with me to the bank tomorrow if you'd like. I wouldn't mind the company."

"I'm glad to help." He led the way back downstairs to his truck. "What time do you want to go?"

"Let's go first thing in the morning. I need to see Mom's lawyer in the afternoon and if there's anything in the safety deposit box for him to handle, I can give it to him then." I managed a credible laugh. "Can you believe it? Ted Otts is Mom's lawyer. Totts. Who would have thought that one of the old gang would turn out to be so respectable?"

Bell smiled. "I knew he had a firm in town. Good old Totts. I'll pick you up at nine, how's that?" Bell glanced at me as he drove. "Or we can go out for breakfast first."

He sounded wistful and a bit hopeful. I suppose it did get boring in town since he didn't know very many people anymore. I know that when I came to visit Mom, she was my main social contact. "You can come over and I'll cook breakfast, then we'll go to the bank."

"Great. I'll be there at nine." He grinned. "I'm

getting tired of my own cooking."

We were quiet for the remainder of the drive. I was lost in thought. It was funny how I remembered the events of that night. So many things had faded into the background of memory, but that night was still so clear.

It was a different time, back when I was a kid. We didn't stay inside playing video games except very late at night. We were outside, wading in the stream and playing pirates. Computers were room-sized contraptions used for complex mathematical computations. The idea of a pocket-sized computer was the stuff of science fiction. The closest we came to "high tech" was a Walkman that played cassette tapes, which we thought was the height of cool.

When we got too old for pirates we still played games but they were the silly dating games of youth. The boys were older than me, but boys and girls mature differently so by the time we were teenagers, we were essentially the same age. I was David's sister and by proxy, I was their sister, too.

Things changed when I got to high school. I was the envy of my circle of girlfriends because I was friends with Peter, Bell, and their buddies, most of whom were the Cool Guys. Bell and I started going steady when I was a sophomore and he was a junior. Somehow it just happened. It seemed natural that he and I would start to date. It was natural that he and I would fall in love.

We were so much alike in many ways and yet so different. He was quick, volatile, and changeable. I was steady, dependable, and predictable. But he had a dependable streak and I had a mischievous streak. We balanced each other in so many ways.

Graduation was a scary time for us. It meant that Bell would be going to university and our simple routines would be changing. College wasn't that far away, so we'd see each other often, but we wouldn't see each daily, the way we did in high school. The party at Jamie Lim's house was the last big blow-out before summer started.

It was on a hot, humid June evening. I can't remember what Bell and I argued about, but I remember the feeling of freedom when I went to the party without him. He and I went steady for two years, doing just about everything together. It was oddly exhilarating to be out without him. He and I had become routine and going to a party on my own was a new experience.

"Peter told you that he and I had a date that night?" I asked, memories percolating in my brain.

"Yeah. In fact, he implied it was more than a date. He said that you and he were going to go steady."

I laughed. "You should have known he was lying. Peter would never go steady with anyone. He was always jumping from girl to girl."

Bell nodded. "In retrospect, I can see what he did. He was setting us both up to believe he was madly in love with you."

I thought of Peter, maybe living in California all these years, living off the money he and his mother got. "That asshole," I muttered.

"Oh, oh," Bell said, leaning forward and staring intently.

"What?" I followed his gaze. A car was parked in front of Mom's house and two men leaned against the doors. One was massively big, like a football player, with a shaved head and arms the size of my thighs. The other was as small as the one was big, with arms that were heavily decorated with bright tattoos. "Who's that?"

"It must be a slow news week. They turn up wherever I go. It could be worse. The word must not be out yet. There'll probably be more tomorrow. These guys aren't so bad. The one with the tats is Billy and the big one is Murphy."

"Who are they?"

Bell let his Ford roll to a stop then he turned off the motor. "Reporters. Wait here."

"What? Why are they—" My words were cut off when Bell got out of the car and went to meet them, the two men hurrying toward him. The big one—Murphy— had a small digital camera and he busily snapped pictures while the other one talked.

I hopped out of the car and hurried to join Bell in time to hear him say, "Hey, guys, come on. We had an agreement."

"Sorry, T.K. This is a big story." The big one alternately focused his camera on me and on Bell while he spoke. The other held out what looked like a small digital recorder, keeping it near Bell's face.

"You're not supposed to bother me in town. You know the rules." Bell held up a hand, effectively blocking the reporter's view of me.

"Come on. Just give us something." The big one turned to me. "What's it like to date one of the richest men in the world?"

I folded my arms and glared at him. "We're not dating. We're old friends."

"What's your name?" Billy, the tattooed one,

demanded.

"None of your damn business. Who are you?"

He smiled, his boyish face creasing to reveal perfect teeth. "Billy Juko. Glad to meet you. Tell us how you and T.K. met."

"I've known him all my life," I said. "We're friends. Just friends. That's all."

"Uh-huh," the big one said doubtfully. "You're Wendy Davis, right?"

"Wendy Davis?" The first man thrust the digital recorder at me. "Is this the woman your app was modeled on, T.K.?

"Are you Wendy Darling?" the other one said.

"What's next for Wendy Darling, T.K.? I heard you're doing a new app."

"One question at a time, one person at a time," Bell said.

"Wait a minute," I protested. "How about no questions?"

"We have to give them a story, Wendy," Bell said patiently. "If we don't, they'll make up something and it'll be worse."

"How could it be worse?"

All three men stared incredulously at me. "Don't you read the tabloids?" Juko asked.

"Of course not. That's just trashy journalism."

"It sells, though." Bell looked at Mrs. Llewellyn who was driving slowly past, eyes glued to us while we stood on the lawn talking. "Let's go inside. Wendy and I will give you a story."

"What story?" I demanded. "And it's my house. I'm the one who does any inviting." They looked expectantly at me. "Oh, okay. Come in." I stalked to the front door, not waiting to see if they took me up on my not-so-gracious invitation.

They were following so closely they almost tread on me when I opened the door. I gestured toward the living room. Athos took one look at the entourage and promptly left the room with a rumbled hiss. I wished I could hiss or join him or both. "I'm not going to offer you any refreshments," I said. "Have a seat."

They plopped down, the two reporters on the couch and Bell in what I thought of as the guest chair, next to Mom's favorite chair. "What do you want?" I asked, glaring at the two men.

Bell held up a hand. "The story is that yes, this is Wendy and yes she's the prototype for Wendy Darling. We're old friends and I'm here to attend her mother's funeral. I was close to her family and her mother died earlier this week."

The men murmured something sympathetic. "You dated in high school and now you're picking up where you left off, right?" the tattooed one said. "It's a big story."

"We're not picking up where we left off," I said. "Look, how old are you?"

"Thirty-three."

I did some mental math. "Okay, imagine that the girl—or boy—you were in love with fifteen years ago showed back up in your life. He or she is rich, successful, and famous."

"He," Juko said almost defiantly, as though I would be shocked he was gay.

"This is Iowa," I said with a dismissive wave of one hand. "You can't surprise me. We've had gay marriage since before it was popular. Say he shows back up in your life and suggests you get together again." I raised a hand when Juko started to speak. "Don't give me any flip answers about how cool it will be to be a kept man or how you wouldn't mind trying out being rich. Think about it." I stared intently at him. "How would you feel?"

To his credit, he pondered it for a second or two. "Obligated," he finally said. "Suspicious. Curious. Why me?"

"Exactly." I turned to Bell. "See?"

Bell shrugged then his demeanor changed. I recognized that look. He was plotting something. "Listen, you guys can help us. A friend of ours died in high school, but now we think he might still be alive. We'd love to get in touch with him."

I stared at Bell, wide-eyed. "What are you—?"

"Just put a mention in the story that Tom Bell and Wendy are hoping they might find out what happened to their old friend, the Shadow." He reached over and took my hand. "It's so important to us."

"The Shadow? Wasn't that like some superhero?" the big guy muttered.

"It's a nickname," I managed to say, trying to tug my hand away from Bell's.

"That's what brought us back together," Bell said with a fatuous smile at me. "We'd like to know what happened."

I could see the romantic wheels turning in the heads of the reporters. "Nice story," Juko muttered.

"Yeah," I muttered, shooting Bell a glare. "What a pity it isn't—"

Bell leaned toward me. "There are always second chances." His pale green eyes seemed to speak worlds.

"It's important that we find what happened to everyone involved, right? I'm sure your mother would agree."

I wavered. He was right but I hated to admit it. I sighed, knowing when I was defeated. "Of course."

"Great angle. Second chances." The big reporter beamed at me. "Thanks for the story."

I managed a weak smile in return. "Glad to help." I squeezed Bell's hand, hard. *I'll pay you back for this,* I mouthed.

He grinned. "I'm counting on it."

Chapter 5

I managed to shoo all of them out of the house without too much more fuss. I watched while Bell and the reporters talked curbside, Bell gesturing toward the house and the two reporters nodding. Lord knows what he was cooking up. I went to the kitchen and poured myself a glass of wine and when I came back to the living room to peek out again, they were all gone.

I sipped the wine while darkness fell and rain moved in, a steady patter interspersed with heavier downpours. The weather had been changeable all spring, with cold spells alternating with heavy rain. The farmers were starting to fret about getting into the fields. It was almost mid-May, which was getting late for planting. A person can't live in Iowa without being aware of the effect of the weather on everything. It seemed like every year farmers worried about too much rain, too much cold, or too much heat. And every year they had bumper crops.

I listened to the rain, the hypnotic sound so relaxing. The stress of my day began to seep out of me, helped along by the wine. I reviewed my eventful afternoon. Fragments of conversation echoed in my brain, mixed with my own speculations. Mom's stroke. Peter might be alive. Jamie Lim was fired. Peter was bisexual. Bell and Peter argued. The old farm.

The phrases all jumbled up in my brain, but one

phrase kept repeating over and over.

"Bell says that…"

Everything we discussed was based on research that Bell or the detective he hired had supposedly done. It was ironic, really. I confronted him about the need for evidence, but I wasn't even questioning his assertions or his motives or his evidence.

I drank one more glass of wine then went to bed, not anxious to pursue that line of thought. My life was already complicated with the reporters who showed up on my doorstep. I'd face my doubts about Bell on the morrow.

It was still raining when I awoke, which squashed my idea of going for a run. My daily exercise routine had been thrown off these last few months so I squeezed in a workout wherever I could. I shelved the idea of a morning jog and resolved to try to get in an afternoon one, instead.

I went downstairs to fix a casserole for breakfast, throwing together whatever I could find from the fridge. At eight o'clock, my phone rang. I expected it to be Bell. I didn't recognize the number on the landline phone display.

"Miss Davis? I'm with the L.A. Tribune. Can you comment on—?"

I slammed the phone down.

Two minutes later it happened again. "Miss Davis? I'm calling from New York. Can you comment on the story in—?"

I slammed it down again.

Two more calls and I quit answering. By the time Bell showed up at the back door, I was ready to whack somebody. When he silently handed me a copy of *USA*

Today folded to the Technology section, I took one look, rolled up the paper, and whacked him with it. "What the hell?" I demanded, shaking the paper at him.

He ducked in mock fear. "It's a good picture."

I unrolled the paper and examined the photo of Bell and me at Peter's grave in a tender embrace. Another photo showed us kissing. "Holy crapola, Bell. Couldn't you bribe them or something?"

"If it's any consolation, my phone has been ringing off the hook." He brandished his smart phone. "Or it would be if it had a hook. Everybody wants a statement."

"Here's a statement for them." I dropped the paper on the couch. "Fuck off."

"Wendy Angela Davis. I am shocked to hear such language from your mouth."

I reached for the newspaper again.

"Okay, okay," he said, holding up his hands. "I'm sorry. Like I said, it must be a slow news week. It will all blow over in a few days."

I fumed while I went back to the kitchen. "They can't show up at Mom's funeral," I stated, taking the breakfast casserole out of the oven. "I insist on that, Bell. I don't care what you have to do, but none of them get within a block of the funeral."

"I promise," he said immediately. "I'll get a restraining order if that's what it takes. That smells good. What is it?"

I dished up two servings on Mom's ceramic plates that I had warming on top of the stove. "Eggs, sausage, some veggies, and whatever else I could find." I handed him one plate then I took the other and the coffee pot with me into the dining room, setting it on a trivet when we sat down.

My cell phone rang while I was pouring a cup of coffee. "Now what?" I muttered. I looked down at the phone number. "I don't know anybody in New York. If it's one of those asshole reporters, I'm going to sue somebody."

Bell looked at my phone display. "I know who it is." Before I could stop him, he answered it. "Wendy's phone. George, is that you?" He sipped his coffee while watching me. "Okay. Here she is." He handed me my phone. "It's my attorney."

I took the phone warily. "This is Wendy."

"Ms. Davis? I'm George Llewellyn, T.K. Bell's copyright attorney. I need some information from you so I can set up the transfer of royalties for the Wendy Darling app to you as T.K. requested."

I thought I sensed faint disapproval in his voice. I could imagine some corporate attorney in a high-rise New York building sneering at Bell's obvious romanticism for assigning me the rights to his app. "What kind of information?" I asked around a bite of food.

"This is great," Bell said, wolfing down his casserole. He ate like a starving man. He probably didn't get much home cooking unless he did it himself and I doubted that. Bell wasn't much of a cook, or at least he hadn't been.

"Glad you like it," I said. "It's easy to do." I realized the attorney was still talking. "I'm sorry, I didn't catch that."

"I said I assume you want the monies direct deposited, so I'll need bank routing numbers and so on. I'll send you a packet of information and once you've filled out everything and signed it, we can get the ball rolling. T.K. insists on doing a lump sum payment for the past five years of royalties, but hereafter you'll receive a deposit every month. Of course, that money won't be for the current month but for several months previous. App stores are notorious for lagging behind in their royalties."

Whatever. Bell was selling WDD for .99, so the royalties probably came to a few hundred bucks or so a month. Well, that was a few dollars I wouldn't object to having. "What kind of royalty percentage is standard for apps?"

Bell wiggled his eyebrows. "Lousy," he muttered.

"Well, there's what's standard, then there's what T.K. Bell can get." The lawyer laughed, a big hearty sound and I revised my mental image of a scrawny Scrooge character to more like Burl Ives or someone equally rotund. "T.K. gets a twenty-percent cut of every sale. And he gets free promo at least four times a year. Wendy Darling has done very well."

It was odd to hear my family nickname bandied about by a stranger. "I told Bell he didn't need to share with me." I glared at the miscreant in question.

Bell stood, holding his plate. "Do you want more?"

I shook my head and took a bite of the casserole. It was pretty good for something I just tossed together at the last minute. Bell vanished into the kitchen as the lawyer said, "Oh, he's not sharing. He's assigning all rights to you. That reminds me. Do you have a lawyer? You probably should have someone review the contract."

Assigning rights to me? Holy crapola. I wonder what that meant. I mentally reassessed the amount I might receive in royalties and upped it by a few hundred. "I have a family lawyer here in town who's settling my mother's estate. I'll ask him if he can do it."

There was a slight hesitation on the other end of the phone. "I don't mean to be disparaging, but handling a detailed software contract might be beyond the scope of a small-town lawyer."

I grinned at his ignorance. "They handle multi-million-dollar farm deals on a regular basis. I think he can review it. If he can't, he probably knows somebody who can." I gave the lawyer Ted Otts' name, address, and phone number, which was jotted on the notepad I habitually carried with me. "Just send everything to him. He can look through all the legal papers and I'll fill them out with his approval."

"I'll fax a copy immediately then courier the originals overnight so your lawyer can review them and there won't be any delay in signing. I know that T.K. is anxious to have this all done immediately. The initial amount might be a bit surprising for your bank, so you may want to discuss it with your account manager."

Account manager? I almost laughed aloud. I kept a two-thousand dollar checking account balance and six-thousand savings balance at my bank in Des Moines. Everything else from my eighty-thousand a year salary was used to pay my mortgage and expenses and whatever was left over was funneled into my 401K or IRA so I could, hopefully, retire before I was too old to enjoy it. "I don't have an account manager at the bank. What kind of figure are we talking about?"

"Well, as I said, the initial deposit will be for back royalties for the five years WDD has been on the market."

"Hmm?" I looked at the kitchen. Bell leaned in the doorway, watching me, his plate in his hand with a big dollop of casserole in the middle.

"Two-hundred-fifty-thousand. Give or take ten thousand."

My mouth dropped open. "Wha—?" I stammered.

"Sales have dropped off slightly, but I think you can expect a minimum of two or three thousand a month for the foreseeable future."

"Seriously?" I asked the lawyer. I looked at Bell. He smiled smugly.

"Oh, yes. I know T.K. is planning a follow-on app, too, for Wendy Darling in college. That promises to be a huge seller. I'm sure you'll have a percentage of that, too, since it's a derivative of the app you have rights to and it uses the same characters."

He continued talking, but it sounded like *blah blah blah* to me. Bell came back into the room and sat down. I handed him the phone. "Why didn't you tell me I'll be rich?"

Bell took the phone. "George? It's me. I think you've stunned Wendy. She can't talk and that never happens, so she must be in shock."

I whapped him on the arm. "Hey."

He fended me off easily and pointed to my plate. "Eat your breakfast before it gets cold. George, she's right. I think you can trust the lawyer here to handle the details. I know him and he's good at what he does."

I tuned him out, eating mechanically while I tried to envision an extra two thousand dollars a month. Holy crapola. It was mind-boggling. I could pay off my condo with the lump sum payment. If I combined the app payments with my salary, I could probably retire in five years, if not sooner. Heck, I could probably retire now if I lived somewhat frugally.

Holy crapola.

I realized Bell had ended the call and was watching me. My happy daydreams began to dissipate when I thought through it all. I set down my fork and stared at him. "Bell, I can't take your money."

"Why not?"

"It isn't right."

He continued eating, unconcerned. "You act like it's illegal or something. It's not blood money. It's all legit."

"But I didn't do anything to earn it."

He was quiet for a minute then pushed his plate away and picked up his coffee mug. "I'm disappointed, Wendy. I didn't think you cared so much about what people think."

"What? It's not that." I pushed my plate away, too, even though I was still hungry. I couldn't eat and focus on being rich all at the same time.

"I heard what you said to Billy Jukes, the reporter. You talked about being a kept woman. Are you afraid that people will think I'm buying your love?"

My cheeks got hot. "It's got nothing to do with that. I don't care what people think. I haven't lived here for decades. What do I care?"

"Then what is it?" When I didn't answer immediately, he said, "It's just money."

"Spoken like a man who has more money than God." I was angry that I was so happy to get so much money. Money represented freedom to me. Bell couldn't understand that.

He looked embarrassed, like he could read my

thoughts. "I didn't set out to get rich. I just wanted to have fun and write programs, like your dad and I did. It was all just good timing and good luck combined with my talent." He wouldn't meet my eyes.

I couldn't argue with that. Bell rode the dot.com wave and he sold his company before the bubble burst for a very good profit. Then he got in on the ground floor of app development. A few of his products had been the forerunners for some of the most successful apps ever.

"I've never seen that much money in one place," I said. "It's just a surprise."

He rolled his coffee around in his mug, looking at it and not at me. "I'm not trying to pry, but what about your mom's estate? Surely there's something there."

"Dad's illness drained most of their savings. After he died, Mom got by on what was left of her savings and Dad's social security. She would never take any money from me. She said she was doing okay."

Bell looked thoughtfully into his coffee mug. "I guess that explains why you only have about one hundred and eighty thousand in your 401K."

I glared at him. "What don't you know about me? I suppose you had a detective researching me, too?"

He avoided that question by saying, "The only thing I don't know is what it will take to convince you I'm sincere."

"I know you're sincere." I stood and picked up my plate, my half-eaten breakfast now cold. "I'm just not sure about your motives."

"My motives?" He looked honestly surprised.

He looked so clueless I decided to mess with him a bit. Two could play the Surprise Game. I leaned over and kissed him so hard I thought I heard his heart stutter. "Motives."

"Love," he stammered, face upraised to me.

"Or nostalgia?" I countered. "Come on."

"Huh?"

"We need to go to the bank." I headed for the kitchen. Bell scrambled to his feet and followed me. "It got better later, you know," I said. "For Mom. She was able to pay off the mortgage when a cousin died and—" I stopped suddenly and turned.

Bell ran into me, jumped back then looked anywhere but at me.

"Bell?" I advanced on him.

He edged past me and set his plate on the counter near the sink. "I admit it. I paid it. It was the least I could do. I owed your father for all he did to get me started."

I whirled and went to the sink, setting my plate into it. I had a hard time not throwing the plate at him. "Damn it, Bell. Am I going to be obligated to you for the rest of my life? Am I?"

He grabbed my arm. "It's only money," he enunciated. "I borrowed from you to design the app. It's only fair that I pay you back."

"You didn't borrow from me—"

He cradled my face in his hands, warm on my cheeks. "Did you cry when your boyfriend hurt your feelings? Did you and a friend spend all day shopping for your prom dress at a consignment store in Des Moines? Did you and your girlfriends go out and TP somebody's house? Were you on the debate team? Did you work on the yearbook?" His eyes were like lasers, extracting memories and feelings long forgotten. "Did you—"

I put my finger on his lips. "Okay, okay. I earned it." I moved away from him and busied myself with covering the casserole and tucking it into the fridge.

"I'll probably end up paying you a consulting fee for *Wendy's College Days*, which I've just started to program." He winked at me. "Maybe we can relive a few old memories while we're at it."

My face got hot at the knowing look in his pale green eyes. My Wendy's college days had occasionally been R-rated. I turned to the sink to rinse the plates, using the action to avoid looking at him. "You know what this means, don't you? I can retire. Like, now, probably."

"Wow. If you're retired, then you'll have plenty of time to consult with me, won't you? Maybe we can do some traveling. And don't forget I want to build that house. I was thinking I'd buy Jamie Lim's old farm. Tear it down and build something there."

"What? That's crazy. Why would you live in Kensington?" I looked at him over my shoulder while I stacked dishes into the dishwasher.

"Why not?" When I started to protest, he overrode me. "It's not far from Iowa City, Cedar Rapids, Des Moines, or the Quad Cities—all the biggest cities in Iowa. It's a four-hour drive to Chicago, a five-hour drive to Kansas City or Minneapolis if I want a bigger city. I can fly my plane here or take the train just about anywhere in the country. It's the best of small town and big city." He looked around the old-fashioned kitchen from his place in the doorway. "I'm tired of smog and traffic jams and earthquakes. I want to come home, Wendy."

The simple sincerity in his voice made me tear up a bit. Heaven knows, I knew how he felt. Des Moines wasn't a metropolis by any means, but there were times when I absolutely hated the traffic, the congestion, and the noise. I turned off the coffee pot and looked around the room for any stray dishes to clean. "Jamie Lim's old house is probably a wreck. Is anybody living there?"

"Nope." Bell leaned against the doorframe, watching me act domestically. "I checked on it. Somebody owned it for twenty years or so, but now the buildings are empty. The land is leased for farming."

"If the house and barn have been vacant then you probably will want to tear it down." I dried my hands on the kitchen towel. "Ready to go?" I looked toward the front door. "I suppose we'll be followed, won't we?"

"Nope." Bell put an arm around my shoulders and led me to the back door. "I've got a deal with them. They leave us alone in town and I report in once a day and give them a story."

"What kind of story?" I grabbed my purse from the small side table near the door. "Athos, take care of things while I'm gone," I called out. The cat didn't bother to reply. He barely looked up from his spot on the couch.

"The kind of story reporters like." When I shot Bell a reproving look, he added, "Nothing untrue. Just that we're getting reacquainted and I'm helping you with the details following your mother's death." He gestured me ahead of him and we emerged into a gentle rain.

"Nothing about romance or stuff like that?" I asked suspiciously while I scrambled into his SUV.

For an answer Bell handed me a manila folder.

"You might find this interesting."

"What's this?" I opened the folder, finding a sheaf of files inside.

"It's a copy of the police report about Peter's death. Or his supposed death." Bell backed the SUV out of the drive.

I noticed a car sitting across the street. "Is that them? The reporters?"

Bell nodded. "I can't stop them from taking pictures. The good thing is that the weather is so lousy, they can't really get anything good." He drove slowly past the dark blue sedan. "Must be a new one. I don't recognize him. I think they're taking turns. Or maybe we're already old news and they've sent in the B-team."

I opened the folder. "How did you get this? Aren't these things confidential or something?"

"Oh, I know a guy who knows a guy." Bell shrugged.

I skimmed through the photocopies of forms, most of them composed on typewriters given the uneven quality of the ink density. There was the dental chart, the small rounded squares of teeth with assorted markings on them denoting fillings, I suppose. Several pages were full of pictures, hard to decipher in the rainy daylight coming into the SUV. "What's this?" I muttered, peering closely at what looked like a tangle of sticks and muck.

Bell glanced at the picture. "The body."

"Yuck." I shoved the page to the bottom of the stack and focused on a one-page summary, signed with a sprawling signature at the bottom of the page. Words jumped out at me. "…followed the tracks to the river, which is approximately a quarter-mile to the south…distraught after arguing with other students…mother stated he was depressed and…"

I closed the folder. "I assume you've read everything here. What's the bottom line?"

"I'm not going to tell you what I think. I want you to read it and tell me what you think. There are few things in there that just don't add up." He turned onto Main Street. "That's one reason I wanted to go to the bank with you. I think your mother might have some answers."

I stared at him, not bothering to hide my shock. "That's crazy, Bell. What could she know about it?"

He parked a few slots away from the Farmer's Mercantile Bank. "Let's find out."

Chapter 6

"What are you saying?" I demanded when he turned off the engine. "You're saying my mother had something to do with Peter's death?"

"I didn't say that. I said your mother might have had some information about it. I think that's why she was asking me so many questions about what happened that night."

I shook my head before he finished speaking. "I'm sure you're wrong. If Mom knew anything about what happened, she would have told me. We talked about it a lot while I was recovering from our car accident. I was so sure that I was the cause of Peter's death. Mom and Dad and I talked about it in the months afterward. I'm sure they didn't know anything about what happened except what we all knew."

Bell took the folder from me and tucked it into the console, which was large enough to accommodate a laptop. "We'll see, won't we? Come on." He didn't wait for my reply, but left the SUV, dashing through the rain to the bank doorway.

"Damn it, Bell," I muttered, following. I met up with him in the front lobby. The old bank had been replaced years ago by this newer, more modern building, interchangeable with any bank in any town in any state. I missed the teller windows with the metal bars, the marble countertops, and the offices with large oak doors behind which your business was completely private. Now it was a glass-and-chrome modern space, cold and impersonal.

We went to the sign-in desk for the vault and were soon escorted by a young female teller back to the safety deposit boxes. I didn't bother to inventory the box, but instead just took out a rubber-banded bundle of paper, several spiral notebooks, one flat envelope, two bulky brown legal-sized envelopes and two small square pasteboard boxes. When the deposit box was empty, I signed the forms relinquishing ownership of the box and turned over the two keys, one that Mom gave me long ago and the other the one I found in the dish on her dresser.

"Do you want a bag for all that?" the girl asked when Bell and I emerged into the lobby.

"I'd appreciate it." I looked at the front window and the rain coming down. "I should have brought one."

"It's hard to think of everything when you're dealing with the death of a loved one," she said sympathetically. "Your mother was the sweetest woman. I enjoyed talking with her when she came in to do her banking. I'll get you a plastic bag. Just hang on a second." She went to the teller area and disappeared into a back office.

"Lightly?" Bell asked, looking at someone behind me. "Is that you?"

I turned and did a double-take. A tall man was emerging from one of the banker offices, hand outstretched and a big smile on his face. Bobby Noble was another one of Peter's gang of Lost Boys. We called him Lightly because he never used to take

71

anything seriously. His fair hair was still wrapped in tight curls on his head and he was still handsome with that cocky grin that seemed to say he knew a secret nobody else did.

"Tom, I heard you were in town." Lightly smiled at me. "Wendy, it's good to see you. I was sorry to hear about your mom. She was one special lady."

I blinked back tears. It was gratifying to know how well-loved Mom was, but it was also hard to bear. It just kept reminding me of how much I already missed her and would miss her far into the future. "Thanks, Bobby." I rearranged the bundle of papers in my arms, one of the notebooks slipping out of my grasp.

Bobby grabbed it before it could reach the floor. "You look overloaded."

"I didn't come prepared for so much stuff. It's been a while since I came down here with Mom to go through the box. I couldn't remember what she had in there." I turned to the girl who hurried across the lobby, holding open a plastic shopping bag.

"That's from your mom's deposit box?" Bobby asked while I tipped the contents of my arms into the bag.

"Thanks," I said to the girl, who smiled and moved away. "Yes, it is. I'm not sure what's in here. I'll go through it all with Totts when I meet with him this afternoon."

"Totts is your lawyer?" Bobby ruffled the pages of the blue notebook he still held. "Funny to think of it, isn't it? I mean, who would have thought Totts would grow up to be a lawyer."

"Who would have thought you'd grow up to be a banker?" I asked. "Or that Bell would become a programmer?"

"Oh, I saw that one coming," Bobby said. "Tom was always tinkering with computers, even back then."

Bell took the notebook from Bobby. "This is one of your Dad's Inspiration Spirals," he said to me, leafing through the yellowed pages. "I remember he was always jotting down ideas, events, his thoughts—whatever sprang into his mind. It's like a combination diary and notepad, all in one. The early version of Evernote, I guess you could say. I did the same thing when I was first getting started designing software code. Your dad would put down an idea and five or six pages later, something else he was thinking about would tie into that first idea. Just like writing code and subroutines. I learned so much from him."

Bobby nodded. "Your father was like one of the kids in a lot of ways, Wendy. I remember those marathon video contests we'd have, holed up in your basement playing games. I always enjoyed running in and out of your house. Your parents sure made us feel welcome. If I can do anything to help, just let me know."

"Thanks, Bobby. I appreciate that. I think I have almost everything under control. I just have to proofread the obituary and go through some pictures, and I think that will do it."

"Speaking of the obituary, that reminds me. I talked to Sylvia Barry the other day."

Bell closed the notebook, giving Bobby his full attention. "Really? What's she up to?"

"She still gets the town newspaper and she read the death notice. She wanted to know if I knew if you'd be in town, Wendy, and for how long. She calls now and then when she sees something in the paper that she's curious about."

"I'm surprised," I said. "You'd think after all this time—and with the bad memories she has—that she wouldn't want to have anything to do with Kensington." I glanced at Bell, but he was once again leafing through the notebook, his face thoughtful.

"She and I exchange Christmas cards and I think, well, I think she's lonely. It doesn't sound like she has a lot of friends in California. Speaking of friends, we should all get together." Lightly looked from me to Bell. "Get the old gang together."

Bell nodded and I knew what he was thinking. Maybe we could pick their brains about what happened. "How about tonight?" I said. "I've got a bunch of cousins coming in to town tomorrow and Friday, but tonight is free. Come on over to the house. Bell can make Mom's pizza. He claims he has her recipe."

"Claim, nothing, I do have it," Bell protested. "Sure, I can whip up dough for a couple of pizzas. You'll see Totts this afternoon and you can invite him. I'll call Dibs and ask him. How about you, Lightly? Can you come by tonight? What about Curly? Is he around?"

"He moved out of state," Bobby said. "The last I heard he was a manager at a building supply company. Are you sure, Wendy? You're probably busy right now. We can go out somewhere. You don't have to entertain us."

I smiled. "I won't entertain you, you guys will entertain me. Come over around five-thirty and we'll have a drink and talk about the old days."

"I'll be there. See you later." Bobby went back to

his office, pausing in the doorway to watch Bell and me while we left.

"Now why would Sylvia be in touch with Lightly?" Bell mused, pausing under the overhang to peer out at the rain. He handed me the notebook and I dropped it into my sack.

"Who knows?" I looked at the steady drizzle. "Ready to make a run for it?"

"I'll race you." Bell dashed out.

I followed more sedately, hampered by my purse and the bag full of Mom's belongings. I fell into the passenger seat, running a hand through my hair and shaking off the rain drops. "Well, that went better than I expected." I set the bag on the floor at my feet.

"What did you expect?" Bell backed out of the parking spot, looking over his shoulder and glancing at me as he did.

"I don't know. More forms to sign or something, I suppose. It seems like all I've done for the past few days is sign papers and accept condolences." I tapped the bag with my foot. "Totts and I need to inventory this because anything in the box is part of the estate."

"Do you think there's anything of value?" Bell made a left turn to head south to the house again.

I took the two jeweler's boxes out of the sack. The name on the box was from a jewelry store in Iowa City, one that hadn't been in business for years. "I doubt it." I opened one box, pulling out a small velvet snap-lid box. I opened it. A plain gold wedding band was tucked into the slot in the yellowed white satin.

The ring was too large for my fingers. "It must be Dad's wedding ring." I opened the other box. It was hard to see the small diamond ring on the white satin through my tears. "This must be Mom's original engagement ring." I twisted the ring I now wore on my right hand, the one with three small sapphires surrounding a ruby. "Dad bought her this ring after us kids were born." I put the boxes back in the sack and stared out my window, tears rolling down my cheeks.

Bell's hand closed over mine. "There are some things of value there, I guess."

"Yes," I said. "There are."

He released my hand and we drove in silence for a minute or two. "Do you want me to help with the notebooks? I'd be happy to read through them. I remember your father and his doodles."

"Sure." I wiped the tears away. "Maybe you can skim them and let me know if there's anything interesting. And don't forget you have to make pizza."

"I've been challenged," he said with a grin. "I won't forget."

My phone chimed from my purse. I fumbled it out and checked the display. "Hello, Aunt Jane. How are you today?"

"Fine. How are you?" There was a note of insistent curiosity in her voice.

"I'm doing okay. I just left the bank. I cleaned out Mom's deposit box."

"That's nice. Loretta at the front desk just showed me a picture of you in the newspaper."

I almost groaned aloud. "I'm so sorry, Aunt Jane. I meant to call you but I've been busy."

"It appears you have been." She sounded amused. "Are you coming over this afternoon so we can go through the pictures?"

"Absolutely," I promised. "In fact, I thought I'd

join you for lunch. Is that okay? I have to meet with Totts at three, so that should give us plenty of time."

"Good. I'm sure we have a lot to discuss." There was definite insistent quality to her voice and I knew I was in for a gentle interrogation.

"I'll see you in an hour or so," I said.

"I have quite a few pictures and some that you may want to use. I'm looking forward to a visit with you."

I ended the call and dropped the phone back in my purse. Jane was my mom's only sister. They had been very close, in touch with each other every day until Mom's stroke landed her in the hospital. Even then, Aunt Jane visited Mom daily because her assisted living apartment was next door to the hospital. I felt guilty that I hadn't kept Jane in the loop on the funeral planning, but she told me to do what I felt was right, so I did and hoped for the best.

"Aunt Jane saw our picture in the paper," I told Bell.

He nodded as though it was the most normal thing in the world. I suppose having his picture in the paper was normal, to him. "It will all blow over in a day or two," he said. "Then we can have some privacy again."

"Privacy? In Kensington?" I shook my head. "This place is gossip central, you know that."

"I guess I should have said privacy in the larger world. I'm serious, Wendy. It's just a slow news week. There will be a few stories in the paper then they'll forget all about us." He turned into the driveway at the house. "Of course, if we get married, it'll be big news again and then we'll just fade away."

"Married?" I grabbed the plastic bag and my purse. "You're crazy, Bell."

"I take it that's a 'no'," he said, drumming his fingers on the steering wheel.

"If that's a proposal, then yes, it's a no." I opened the car door. "Don't forget to call Dibs about tonight. See you later."

"Wendy."

I hesitated. "What?"

"I'm serious."

I stared into his eyes. "So am I." I left, slamming the door behind me, not sure if I was angry, sad, or a combination of the two. I dashed into the house and walked down the hall to the living room, my erratic emotions bouncing like the bag slapping against my leg.

What right did Bell have to come back into my life? Where was he when my brother died? When my father died? He was off gallivanting around the world, earning millions.

Millions which he did share with my mother by paying off her mortgage and probably helping her financially in other ways. I had to be fair. Maybe he did help Mom because he felt bad that he hadn't been around when Dad died or maybe he had some other motive.

It couldn't be love for me, I was pretty darn certain about that. It was ridiculous to think that Bell would still love me after all these years. I had read all the stories in the newspapers about him and various women. Most of them were models or actresses, women who were accustomed to the kind of jet-set life he led.

I sank onto the couch next to Athos, who dozed in his favorite spot. All kinds of crazy emotions were boiling around inside me. I resented Bell coming back into my life. I was grateful for the money he was giving me and I was pissed off that I was grateful. I didn't want to love anybody. I was happily single. I didn't want to live on a farm in Kensington. I had a perfectly good condo, I had friends, I had a life somewhere else.

I patted the cat, who purred happily. "It's silly," I muttered. "Bell can't be lonely. He can't love me."

Athos stretched, but he had no answers for me. "Things will work out or they won't," I muttered, opening the bag and pulling out the bundle of papers and the overstuffed envelopes.

One fat envelope contained a stack of savings bonds, most in small denominations. I would need to tally those and see what they were worth. The other big envelope had a copy of Mom's will, a copy of Dad's will, copies of their Living Wills as well as a copy of my will which I had given to Mom years ago. I set it aside, making a mental note to update my own will. Mom had been my beneficiary, but now that she was gone, I'd need to decide on someone else.

I stared into the dark TV. I would have some real money to leave now that Bell was assigning the rights to the app to me. Who would I leave my estate to? I considered my options. I had no close living relatives. My brothers were dead and now both parents were dead.

I was an orphan.

It was odd to phrase it like that, but it was true. I was alone in the world. Oh, I had cousins and I had friends, but I had no true connection to anyone.

Except Bell, if I chose it.

I considered that thought for a long moment. Bell must have felt like this most of his life. His father was absent and Bell was more mature than his mother had ever been. As soon as he could, he left and it sounded like he and his mother parted ways without a backward look.

Peter, too, had an absent father but he and his mother had a different relationship. In many ways, Peter was the grown-up and Sylvia was the teenager because she was far more concerned about social status than he was. Sylvia always wanted to be part of the In Crowd in Kensington, such as it was, while Peter didn't seem to care. I remember a few times when he called her when we were out late. He always said it was so she wouldn't bug him when he got home, but I think he knew she might worry.

Or maybe he was checking up on her. The thought sprang into my head when I remembered how she loved to party, going to every function at the Country Club and oftentimes chairing the committee that ran the events. Memberships were relatively inexpensive, but still a stretch for a woman living on alimony. Peter worked after school and once told me that he felt like he never had a childhood because he had to be the grown-up after his father left.

No wonder Peter and Bell gravitated toward my parents, who were always there, always willing to listen, always willing to have kids underfoot. My mother checked each kid's report card, my father listened and gave advice when a boy had a crush on a girl, and both of them instilled in all of us a sense of right and wrong that persisted to this day.

Well, they *tried* to instill that sense. If Bell was right, they failed with Peter. I set the legal documents to one side and picked up the stack of papers. It was about an inch thick and was rolled up from being bound by a rubber band. I re-rolled it in the opposite direction and it lay relatively flat on my lap.

More legal documents. Dad's discharge papers from the Army. The paid-off mortgage on the house, the realty papers from when they purchased the house, birth certificates for us kids, death certificates, social security paperwork—more forms, more paper to prove someone had lived, someone had died.

I put it aside with the wills and opened the flatter envelope. A small key fell out and bounced between two couch cushions. I retrieved it and some cookie crumbs. It was an odd little key on a neck chain, like a replica of a big skeleton key, with an oversized flat acorn at the top, making it easy to grasp.

I pulled out a letter.

Wendy Darling—

I smiled at my pet name, the one that Bell had used in his app and the nickname my parents used since I could remember.

Wendy Darling, I lied to you. It's time you know the truth.

The papers rightfully belong to you. I kept them secret, at first because I wanted to protect you. Then, later, I think I wanted to protect myself because I kept them secret.

Does a day or a week or a month less matter? I don't know any more. The key is to my treasure chest. Now, finally, you can have it.

Your Aunt Jane knows some details. I asked her to share them with you if you ask. See her when you can and she'll help fill in the holes.

I love you and all that we did was done to spare

you pain. I don't know if I did that—or did I only postpone it?

Love,
Mother

The "treasure chest" was a wooden box, about a foot long and six inches wide and high. It was a replica of a classic "hope chest," like the big cedar chest that held our blankets in the downstairs bedroom. Mom's treasure chest sat on her dresser and when I was a little girl, I could play with it and the costume jewelry inside.

Then, later, she got a lock for it and I never saw it opened again. I asked her about it once, when Dad died and she was getting ready for the funeral. "I lost the key," she said.

"I could probably open it for you," I said, looking at the cheap lock. "Dad has some metal snips in the garage. I'll bet I could—"

"If I wanted it open, I would have had your father do it. It's fine as is." She pulled out a handkerchief from the drawer and handed it to me. "Here. I'm sure you'll need this today."

Her brusque answer surprised me, but we were both grieving and I didn't think any more about it. We had a funeral to get through and then I went back to college. And a couple of years later there was another funeral for my brother and then another for my other brother who died overseas. The treasure chest sat on her dresser, unopened, and I forgot all about it—until today.

I went into the downstairs bedroom where Mom and Dad had slept for years. The small chest was on the dresser, as always. The key fit the padlock and when I inserted the key, the lock turned easily, as though it waited all those years for me.

The little box was full of folded papers. On top was the newspaper clipping.

Local Boy Dies in Tragic Accident
I pulled out the papers and began to read.

Chapter 7

Two hours later, I faced my Aunt Jane across the miniscule kitchen table in her apartment, one of many in the assisted living tri-story building on the east side of town. Her living quarters consisted of a tiny galley kitchen with the table wedged into one corner, an equally small living room, and a generously sized bedroom with attached bathroom. It was small but pleasant with a view of the flower gardens outside and the leafy trees being watered by the steady rain that continued to fall.

Jane's husband died shortly after they were married. She had lived in Chicago most of her adult life, returning to Kensington fifteen years earlier to retire and be near Mom, her younger sister. The two ladies had a very active social life until Mom's illness hospitalized her earlier in the year. They golfed up until a few years ago, played in several different bridge clubs, and volunteered their time at many civic events. If Jane ever missed her life as an executive secretary to the head of a big corporation, she never mentioned it.

My aunt was a tall woman, taking after my grandfather who was six-foot tall and not my grandmother, who was five-foot tall. Jane's white hair was still thick and bundled into a fat braid that was wound into a twist at the back of her head. She'd worn her hair that way since I could remember and once I wanted to have such luxurious, waist-long hair myself. I tried it briefly and realized I wasn't cut out for the maintenance. When I told Jane that, she laughed. "It's not a matter of style but convenience," she told me. "I don't know how else to fix my hair."

Even now, with eyesight limited due to macular degeneration, her hair was tidy and neat. I ran a hand through my own cropped style and envied her the ability to keep up appearances. I could hope for so much when I was her age. "Bell told me that reporters would get tired of us and move on to another story in a day or two," I told her in response to the newspaper she showed me.

"It's a great romantic story," Aunt Jane said, fiddling with her fortune cookie. The remains of the take-out Chinese meal I brought were on the table between us.

"Romance my foot," I muttered. "They're just looking for something about Bell. He's a big enigma to them."

"Tom Bell is a quandary," she agreed. "He's a man who appears to be completely at home being alone. Then he finds you again and look what happens. Now he's a man like any other man, one who apparently wants to have a woman in his life. It's a great story in what is probably a slow news week."

"Bell said the same thing about a slow news week. And he hasn't found me. I was never lost. It's all a tempest in a teapot."

"But you and he are an item, aren't you?"

"Of course not. He's just feeling nostalgic. Or something." I crumbled my own fortune cookie and read the inscription. *Your true love awaits you.* "Oh, for cryin' out loud," I muttered, tearing it up.

"What?"

"Nothing. All I meant is that Bell is retiring and he's at loose ends."

"And one of those loose ends is you?" Before I could reply, Jane continued. "Look at it this way. What if you had just met him? What if he was a new person you didn't know and you were attracted to him? You are attracted to him, aren't you?" she asked, her thin hands deftly extracting the paper from her cookie.

"I—I suppose so," I stammered. The question caught me by surprise. He was Bell. There wasn't a question of was he attractive. He was Bell.

"Well, pretend he's someone you've just met. Forget about the money and the fame and all that. Do you like him? Does he have qualities you admire and respect?"

"Yes," I said reluctantly. "But there's the past and—"

"Forget that," she said with a wave of her hand.

The fortune from her cookie landed near me and I picked it up, rolling it into a tight little spiral. "It's hard to forget," I said. "He and I have a lot of past together."

"Look at it this way. Do you believe in love at first sight? Or something like it?"

"I'm not sure."

"I do. I think some people are meant to be together. I think you and Tom belong together. You're opposites but you're so much alike."

I smiled at this odd description. "How can that be?"

"He's silly in ways you aren't and you're silly in ways he isn't. He's serious in ways you aren't and you're serious in ways he isn't. You fit together so well. What's my fortune say?"

"Hmm?" She had exactly summarized my own evaluation of how Bell and I were alike and different. Was it so obvious?

"My fortune. What's it say?" Jane gestured toward the paper I held.

I unrolled it. "Great things await those you love." I shredded it and added it to the shreds that were my own fortune.

"See," she said triumphantly. "What did I tell you?"

"Great things could equate to all kinds of things. Not necessarily love." I considered telling her about Bell handing over the rights to his app, but I decided not to open that can of worms and reinforce her faith in the fortune cookie.

Jane toyed with the remains of her cookie, breaking off little shards of it. "You said you emptied out your mother's safety deposit box."

I nodded then realized she probably couldn't see me clearly. "We did. Today."

"We?"

I sighed. "Bell and I."

"Did you find the letter?"

"Yes. Mom said that you'd fill me in."

"Let's go into the living room and sit down."

Going into the living room was just a few steps away in her tiny apartment. I picked up the paper plates and disposed of them, then tucked the leftover food into the fridge for her to have some other time. By the time I finished that, Jane was settled into her favorite armchair in the corner of the room near the window. I took a seat on the couch nearby and picked up the box of photographs she had brought out when I arrived. "Are these the pictures you wanted me to go through?"

"There might be a few in there that could be used for the service. I have a lot of pictures of your mother and father when they were younger."

I looked down at one such picture on top of the stack. My parents were a very handsome couple in their youth. Of course, my father didn't live long enough to get old, having died when he was in his forties, but my mother had retained a fragile prettiness into old age.

"Your father saw Peter Barry the night he supposedly died," Aunt Jane said without any preamble or introduction.

"Where did he see him?"

"It was your father's bowling night. He was driving home from the Lanes. He saw Peter Barry walking across a field near the road." Jane waited expectantly for me to ask the next logical question.

'The Lanes' were a bowling alley and roller rink on the outskirts of town. They were situated on the same road that led to Jamie Lim's old farm, the one that Bell was thinking about buying and the farm where we had the graduation party on the night Peter disappeared. "What time did he see him?"

Jane nodded, pleased that I asked the right question. "I'm not exactly sure. This is all speculation, you understand. I wasn't here then. Your mother called me when you were injured and I came out here to help. Your parents spent most of the time at the hospital with you and with Tom, and I made sure the boys got to school and got fed."

I didn't remember any of that. My hospital stay

after our car accident was a hazy blur in my memory. "If it's all speculation, why bring up the past?"

"Your mother came to me several years ago. She was going through your father's belongings and she found one of those notebooks he kept. He wrote something that made your mother wonder if Peter went to the river, the way the police insisted he did."

I thought of the Inspiration Spirals, now with Bell. "Mom copied a bunch of notebook pages and had them in that little chest she kept on her dresser."

"Those must be the pages she was talking about."

I was shaking my head before Jane finished speaking. "I looked through them. I didn't see anything from that night."

Jane tapped the arm of her chair, lips pursed in thought. She looked like a regal bird of prey, trying to decide where next to cast her gaze and search for an unsuspecting meal. "I think your father talked to Sylvia Barry. That was the impression your mother gave me. Remember, everything was sort of crazy then. You'd been in an accident and were in the hospital and your parents were in a tizzy about that. Your father wasn't sure what to do. If he went to the authorities and claimed Peter was still alive, how could he prove it? Then when the body was found, he decided he must have been mistaken. I think he was trying to protect you. I think he didn't want rock any boats."

"That's ridiculous," I snapped, angry that I was being cast as a cause for my father's concern. "If Dad knew something, he should have gone to the police, not to Sylvia."

"He was already ill, Wendy. Or at least, he wasn't fully well. Back then, men didn't go to the doctor unless there was something obviously wrong. He was tired, with bouts of dizziness and nausea."

She was right. Dad was sick for years before his throat cancer was finally diagnosed.

"And he was worried, I suppose. Your parents were never very financially secure and it wore on him."

She wasn't telling me anything I didn't know. Dad was a lawyer but he didn't have wealthy clients. As cruel as it sounds, it may have been fortunate that my brother John didn't want to go to college and that my brother Mike died when he did. Otherwise my parents would have had three kids in college, a monetary burden that would have overwhelmed them.

"He went to Sylvia Barry a day after Peter disappeared, thinking he could ease her mind. Remember, as far as anyone knew, Peter had run away. It took a day or two before the police thought he might have gone to the river. Instead of being relieved, she put the blame squarely on you and on Tom Bell." Jane shook her head disapprovingly. "Your father loved Tom Bell as much as he loved his own children. He and Tom were kindred souls. That's why he never said anything more about it."

"It all depends on what time Dad saw Peter," I said slowly. "I think Peter and I argued right when it was getting dark. I remember seeing him silhouetted in the window at the barn. The sun was setting, and all I saw was his outline." Then he jumped. I ran to the window to look out, but Bell called my name and I went to the ladder instead, scrambling down out of the loft to meet him. I never saw Peter again.

"Your parents always hoped you and Tom would settle down together."

Jane's quiet statement drew my thoughts away from the past to the here and now. How odd it would be if my parents' hope would come true years later. "They never said anything to me about it," I said, sifting through the photographs in the box.

"They didn't want to influence you. They loved Tom. He was special to them, more than the others. Your mother never liked Peter. She said he was sly. He was too self-centered." Jane waved one graceful hand as though dismissing Peter. "I didn't know him or the others very well, but I got to know Tom when you were injured."

Mom was right in her assessment of Peter. He was the center of his world and the rest of us were satellites that revolved around him. I looked at the picture on top of the others in the box. It was me, Bell, Peter, and his girlfriend, Tina. My brothers and their girlfriends were off to one side. We all wore shorts and the boys were bare-chested. Tina and I wore halter tops, our shoulders brown from the sun. We were grouped around a kiddie pool in the back yard, our feet in the pool.

"Our beach," I whispered. "Dad put in a big sand box and we put that wading pool smack in the middle. Dad called it our private beach."

"They wanted to give you so much but they just couldn't. I suppose all parents feel that way, but your parents pretty much raised Tom and Peter, too. It was a strain on them, financially."

I set the photo aside in the "Me" stack, not the "Mom" stack. "They did fine. We didn't miss being richer." The clock ticked loudly on the bookcase, checking off the seconds. I was suspended in time, somewhere between childhood and adulthood. Behind me was childhood, when Bell was a friend and life was simple. Ahead of me was adulthood, with Mom and Dad gone and Bell—

I raised my head and stared, unseeing, at a picture on the wall. Bell had always been there. He was a part of my life since my earliest childhood. I think I always loved him. Back when I first met him, I was only eight years old and I had a terrible crush on him.

As we both got older, that crush evolved into something more lasting, until he became a fixture in my life. He was mercurial and changeable, and yet he was always constant in his unfailing devotion to my family and to me. He was always in my life until we parted when I was in college.

I had been searching for a replacement, all these years. I'd been looking for someone who was a friend as well as a lover. I never found anyone. The knowledge washed over me.

"The police didn't want to call it a suicide. Sylvia insisted on that. When the body was found, she went into a tailspin."

Once again, I was pulled back to the present and my thoughts dissipated, all but a vague feeling of *rightness.* I had discovered an essential truth. I filed it away for later evaluation.

"You can see how it must have looked to someone who didn't know the people involved very well," Jane said. "Sylvia said that you and Bell teased and bullied poor Peter." Her voice dripped with disdain. "Your parents were, oh, I guess they were naive. Your father hesitated. And Sylvia made sure he knew what might happen to you if he went to the police."

"I was in the hospital. I didn't know any of this

was happening."

"I didn't find out some of it until years later. By then it was all blown over. It was all called an accident. You went off to college, Tom Bell was in college, your father was dying, and your mother was—she was—" Jane sighed. "She had too much to deal with."

I looked down at the next photo on the stack. It was a grainy color print of me and Bell. I sat cross-legged in the open trunk of a car, his coat around my shoulders. He stood nearby, laughing, with a beer in one hand and a cigarette in the other. His hair was thick and long, falling into his eyes. It was Homecoming at college. I remembered it. We spent a party weekend at his apartment. It was the first time I was at a real college event and I loved every minute of it.

"And now we're revisiting it," I said. "It's all coming back to haunt us. Why?"

"Haunt? No, not that. It's come back to awaken us, maybe." She regarded me, her head tilted to one side so she could catch a glimpse of me through her damaged dark blue eyes. "What really happened that night?"

"Peter and I argued and he jumped out the barn window. That's all I know. You should talk to Bell. He's convinced Peter didn't die."

"You see." Jane pounced, reinforcing my image of a bird of prey. "What if your father had proof that Peter didn't die that night?"

"He didn't have proof." I quickly sorted more of the photographs. I looked at one of my father and mother, so young and carefree.

"But—"

"I'll send Bell over to talk to you." I picked up the two stacks of photos, leaving the rest in the box. "You guys can talk conspiracy theories to your hearts' content." That reminded me of something Bell had said. "You said someone visited Mom the day she had her stroke. Do you know who it was?"

Jane tapped the chair arm again, her eyes narrowed in thought. "She just said it was an old friend who came to call. I assumed it was Tom Bell because he often visited her. You knew that, didn't you?"

"Yes." I knew it after the fact, but Jane didn't need to know that.

"When I called her again, she didn't feel well. I took her to the hospital and they discovered she had a heart attack. That night she had her stroke and…" Jane's voice trailed away.

I was reminded, once again, that my mother's death affected many more people than just me. My mother was Jane's only remaining relative, too. Their other sibling, my uncle, had died five years earlier in a car accident. "Mom's illness came as a shock to me, too."

Jane waved away my sympathetic murmuring. "I talked to Tom later and he said that it wasn't him. So who visited her?"

"Bell thinks somebody caused her stroke," I said dismissively. "For heaven's sake, how could somebody do that? I mean, Mom had a heart attack then she had the stroke when she was in the hospital."

"I've been thinking about that." Jane fumbled in the little cloth organizer with pockets slung over the chair arm. "I did some research about various poisons. If somebody visited her and they poisoned her, it might look like a heart attack and it would later cause a stroke. There are several different things that can be used to do that."

I stared at her, open-mouthed. "How did you do research?" I finally managed to ask. "You can barely see the television set, much less a book."

"I know how to dial a phone number," she retorted. "And I know the phone number of the public library. There are people there who are paid to do research."

I almost groaned. Holy crapola, what would the librarian think?

As though reading my mind, Jane said, "I told her I was in a book club and we were arguing about a plot point that was too vague in the book we were reading. I asked her if she could find out if there's an easily accessible poison that could cause a heart attack and/or a stroke." Jane smiled triumphantly at me.

"And did she?"

"She did indeed." Jane flourished a piece of paper. "You just take that to Tom Bell and see what he thinks."

I set the box of photos on the couch and crossed the room to take the paper, adding it to the two sets of photos I was taking with me. I glanced at the handwriting, loopy and large, but I couldn't quite figure out what it said. "I'll have Bell give you a call if he has any questions."

"You sound doubtful, but you shouldn't be. Peter Barry was a sly, conniving sort of boy. That's what your mother said. You listen to what Tom Bell says."

I bent over and kissed Jane's cheek. "I'll give this to Bell and we'll see what he can make of it. If anybody can figure it out, he can. The cousins are coming in tomorrow. We'll all get together for dinner, okay?"

Jane sighed resignedly. "David's children are so

noisy. Are they bringing along any of their spawn?"

I laughed. "I doubt it. The younger generation isn't much interested in family."

"Well, that's something at least. Call me tomorrow and let me know what time to be ready. Are your father's relatives coming, too?" She stood and walked with me to the door.

"Yep, they're coming on Friday. We'll have a full house for Mom." I hugged Jane and she returned the hug, almost squeezing the breath out of me.

"You listen to Tom, you hear me?" she whispered into my ear. "He's a smart boy."

"Too smart for his own good, sometimes." I pulled away and kissed her again. "I'll talk to you tomorrow."

"Just because I sound paranoid that doesn't mean someone isn't out to get me." She smiled. "Isn't that the truth, sometimes?"

That was almost exactly what Bell had said.

Chapter 8

On my drive to Totts' legal office downtown, I thought about what she said. Both Bell and my aunt seemed to think that foul play was involved in Mom's illness. I trusted them and knew that Jane, at least, was a level-headed, calm person.

Was there something to what they thought? How could someone have poisoned my mother? Wouldn't the hospital discover it when she was admitted? I assumed they would do blood work and other tests, so if something odd showed up, they would be alerted, wouldn't they?

Maybe more to the point, *why* would someone do it? Mom had her heart attack on February second and her stroke just a day later, when she was still in Intensive Care. She had initially been disoriented and almost manic, then she had fallen into periods of anxiety, like panic, asking me over and over if the house was locked, if she had her keys, if the car was parked in the right location and other inconsequential questions.

Her stroke happened when I was out of her room, taking a break and eating lunch in the hospital cafeteria. When I came back, the room was full of hospital staff around her bed, alerted by the monitors that went off when her respiration and oxygen levels changed. Her primary doctor told me it wasn't unusual for a heart attack victim to have a stroke, but he seemed surprised by it, especially because she was recovering so well after her heart attack.

I needed to think about that later. Right now I had a lawyer to talk to. I parked outside Totts' office and dashed inside through the rain with the bag from the bank. The secretary ushered me to his private office and I dropped into the guest chair in front of his large oak desk.

Ted Otts was a big man, not only overweight but big-boned. He'd been a linebacker on the football team and he still had the broad shoulders and big chest of the farm boy he'd been. "How are things going, Wendy? Everything set for the funeral?" He pulled over a fat accordion folder, the one containing Mom's paperwork.

"I just have to drop off some pictures and that should be done. We've got the music figured out, the memorial fund set up, and a couple of people volunteered to speak during the service." I suddenly wondered if Bell would like to speak. I made a mental note to ask him when I saw him later. That reminded me. "Tom Bell is in town and we ran into Lightly at the bank. We're all getting together tonight at Mom's house. Can you join us?"

"I'd like that." Totts glanced at this desk calendar, one of the old-fashioned kinds on a spindle with a page per day. "What time?"

"Cocktail hour. Bell is going to make pizza."

"Are you sure we won't be intruding?" He folded his large, blunt-fingered hands on top of the file and regarded me over the top of his half-glasses. His face was lined from years in the sun, probably on the golf course and his skin had a coarse, papery look. Totts had always been an avid sportsman and spent every free moment he could outdoors.

"I'd like the distraction." I opened the plastic bag and set the papers and the jewelry boxes on the desk. "These were in the safety deposit box. Some savings bonds, a few legal papers, and some jewelry. There were some notebooks of Dad's, too, but Bell has those. He wanted to look through them. You know how Dad was always jotting down ideas for inventions and games."

Totts smiled. "Your parents were so great with us kids. I remember I talked to your dad once about what I should do after graduation. I had an idea that maybe I could get into computers, but he convinced me that wasn't for me."

I wasn't surprised. Totts didn't have the flair for math that my father, Bell, and Peter had. Odd. I'd forgotten that. Peter was something of a math savant, with the ability to solve complex equations in the blink of an eye.

"My family wanted me to go to Iowa State and major in Agriculture," Totts continued, "but I always thought your dad had such a cool job, being a lawyer. When I said that, he said that being a lawyer was a lot like being a game designer. You need to figure out what makes people tick then figure out how to use that to your advantage." He grinned, small fans radiating out from the corners of his pale blue eyes. "It sounded like fun to me."

Odd again. I had never considered whether my father liked what he did. I suppose in many ways the Lost Boys were closer to him than I was.

Totts' smile faded and he started sorting through

the papers. "And it gives me a chance to help people and I like that. I think you can file most of these papers. I'll find out the values on the bonds and add it to the estate total. I doubt if the jewelry is worth much monetarily, but I'm sure they're valuable to you for sentimental reasons if nothing else."

"Bell said the same thing," I murmured.

"Well, he would, wouldn't he?" Totts jotted notes on the legal pad next to him. "Tom always did have a good sense for what was really important in life, like family and friends. Say, that reminds me." He picked up a manila file folder from the In Basket on his desk and slid it across the surface to me. "This was faxed to our office today. The cover note said that I was supposed to review it, at your request, so I did." He regarded me with a wry smile, peering over his glasses. "Looks like you'll be coming into some money."

I took the folder, my face getting hot. "Bell insists on sharing the app royalties with me."

"Oh, he's not sharing. He's giving the app to you, completely. It's only fair. The app is named for you and it's based on your whole high school life." Totts frowned. "In fact, you probably should have sued him a long time ago. If you'd like, we can consider that. Maybe he owes you back interest for—"

I held up a hand. "Please. No lawsuits. What he's doing is fair. Bell did all the work."

"But you provided the inspiration." Totts smiled. "Of course, you always were Bell's inspiration." He returned his attention to the papers in front of him, missing my astonished look. "I'll have a preliminary tally on the estate for you by Friday. It will be awhile before all the bills and so on are paid, so we won't have a final summary for some months. I'm sure there's more than enough in her investment account to pay any outstanding debts."

"What?" I was a joint signee on all of Mom's accounts and the last time I checked, she only had a few thousand dollars in the bank.

"Her investment account. She has about a hundred thousand there."

My mouth sagged open. "What investment account?"

"Ah. Yes." Totts leafed through the papers in front of him and pulled out a page filled with numbers. "Here you go. My preliminary Preliminary Estimate, I guess you could call it."

I skimmed over the figures on the page. By his tally, Mom had almost one-hundred-fifty thousand dollars in various accounts. "Where did she get…?" The words died on my lips. "Bell."

"Maybe." Totts nodded.

My hand holding the paper trembled so much I couldn't read the words. "Every time I turn around, he's involved in my life. Even in death, he's involved." Tears filled my eyes. I wasn't sure if it was anger, frustration, or amazement, but I do know that if Bell had been there, I would probably have hit him.

"He cares about your family, Wendy. He didn't have much family of his own. This"—Totts gestured to the paper I held and the manila folder with the app information—"all of this is his way of helping his family. Let him."

I struggled to my feet, my knees so shaky they felt like rubber. "I guess I don't have much choice, do I? He's going to help me no matter what I do. Thanks,

Totts. I'll see you tonight. Any time after five-thirty is good."

"Wendy—"

"I'll see you later." I left before he could offer any other defense of Bell. I wasn't sure I wanted to hear it. I wasn't sure what I felt or what I wanted except to have a chance to get away and try to put it all in perspective.

I don't remember walking out of the office or getting into my car, but I must have because the next thing I was aware of was driving through town, making random turns on various streets as I struggled to process what Totts said. The rain had changed to a fine mist, which matched what I was feeling: fogged and unclear about everything. Too much was happening for me to understand it.

I remember one time when I complained to Mom about being inundated with tasks at work. "Just line 'em up and take 'em one at a time," she advised. "You'd be surprised. Once you get one knocked off, a lot of the other ones don't look so big."

She was right. I needed to take things one at a time.

1. Bell had supported my family in the past and would be supporting me, indirectly, in the future. There was nothing I could do about either, so I crossed that off my Worry List.

2. Bell thought Peter was still alive. There was nothing I could do about that, so I crossed it off my list.

3. Bell thought he was in love with me. Only time would tell. Nothing to do now, so cross it off my list.

4. I had to get organized for Mom's funeral. Now there was something I could do.

I turned and headed for the funeral home on the east side of town. I took the stack of pictures from Aunt

Jane and the others I had brought from home and went inside, dodging raindrops. The funeral home was an old white Victorian mansion, complete with turret towers and ornate woodworking around each window. The portico over the front door was where the hearse departed for the drive to the cemetery, not far away.

I gave the photos and the obituary to the funeral director and spent a few minutes with their media specialist, a boy who looked high school age and was probably chairman of the AV Club there. My mother had been a great fan of the Beatles, so it was decided to use *The Long and Winding Road* as the musical background for the slide show the boy would put together.

"We've received some cards from out of town people," the funeral director said when I was preparing to leave. He handed me a beribboned bundle of about a dozen cards. "A lot of times people will see the notice in the newspaper, but they don't know the address of a loved one, like you. So the cards come to us."

"Thank you. Do you need anything else from me?"

"No, I think that's all we'll need. I tucked the list of people who asked to speak in with the cards. Let me know if there are any changes you want to make."

What a tactful person, I thought while I hurried back to my car. *Any changes I want to make.* In other words, is there anybody on that list that you don't want to speak? I shook the rain from my hair and started to drive home then I realized I had a houseful of guests coming soon. I had a fridge full of donated food, but I should stop at the grocery store and get some wine, beer, and mix. My cousins were a thirsty lot.

By four-thirty I was home and the groceries were

stowed. I tossed the stack of cards on the credenza in the dining room and busied myself with setting out glasses, silverware, plates, and a platter of chips and dip. I dished out some food for Athos and scooped his litter box then ran upstairs to my room and quickly changed into a clean pair of capris, a blue-and-green striped knit top, and sandals. I dabbed on a smidgen of makeup then came downstairs.

I went to the small CD player in the corner of the living room and sorted through the drawer of CDs in the container under the player. Mom had an assortment of music from the Sixties and Seventies and a scattering of tunes from later than that. I pulled out a Greatest Hits compilation and it was then I saw several CDs I didn't expect to see—Death Cab for Cutie, Coldplay, Nickleback, Duffy.

Then I saw a CD in a jewel case with no cover, just a plain white piece of paper tucked into the case. I took out the paper and read the playlist, all written in Bell's distinctive miniscule handwriting.

Rolling in the Deep, by Adele; *Breathe,* by Anna Nalick; *The Rising,* by Springsteen; *If Everyone Cared*, by Nickleback; *I Will Follow You Into the Dark*, by Death Cab; *True Companion,* by Marc Cohen.

There were more songs, all songs that I loved, all songs I played often. It was as if Bell put together a playlist that I would listen to, again and again.

How did he know?

Again, I had that feeling of epiphany, that sense of *rightness*. He knew because he knew me. Separated across time and distance, he knew what I would enjoy. He had put together a playlist and shared it with my mom, the other person who would hear those songs and know why they were my favorites. I wondered when he did it for her.

I sat back on my heels, the CD in my hand. How could he have known? That playlist was so similar to the one I had on my phone. It was as though Bell spied on me and knew exactly what I loved. Then I thought about the app. It was the same thing. He had *known*, with unerring and unnerving accuracy, how I felt in high school, what I experienced, what I cared about and what frightened me.

I wasn't sure I liked knowing there was a person in the world who knew me so well.

I spied Mom's small digital camera, sitting on the table next to the player. With just a little bit of fumbling, I looked at the last few photographs she had taken. There was one of Bell, sitting at the lake and throwing bread to the pelicans. Someone had taken a picture of the two of them with pelicans not far away, the trees bright with autumn color.

There was one picture of Mom that made my throat tighten. She sat on a picnic table, looking out at the lake. A pelican was on the ground near her feet, also looking at the lake as though mimicking her. She looked pensive and sad, her eyes on the distant horizon.

Another was of the two of them, Bell with his arm around her shoulders and Mom laughing at whoever was taking the picture. There was snow on the ground and it looked like they stood near the motel where Bell had his apartment.

Every time I turned around, Bell was in my life. I hadn't seen him in a decade and then it was very briefly, but it felt as though he had never left. I put the CD and camera back in their places and went to the sideboard in the dining room to mix myself a drink.

Perhaps number three on my list of things to think about would need to be re-thought. Yes, Bell thought he was in love with me.

Was I in love with him? Or was I in denial?

"Two pizzas, coming up," Bell said, coming in the back door and flourishing two plastic-wrapped pans of pizza. I followed him into the kitchen to inspect his efforts. One appeared to be multi-cheese and the other had sausage, red peppers, and mushrooms. "I followed her recipe to the letter. They're ready to go in the oven." He set the pans on the kitchen counter and we went back to the sideboard in the dining room. "That looks good. Mix me one?"

I splashed ginger ale and bourbon into a glass with ice and handed it to him. "Totts said he was would come over."

"And Dibs is coming, too." Bell sipped his drink and peered out the side window. "I was right. That is a new reporter. I tried to talk to him earlier but he took off before I could get close. The other guys don't know who he is."

I ducked under Bell's arm and peeked outside. The dark blue sedan was parked across the street. "I thought you had a deal with them."

"I have a deal with the regular ones. I don't know who this one is." Bell stepped away from the window and looked down at the stack of sympathy cards. "If he files a story I don't like, I'll sue the media company he's with, so it's not a problem."

"Of course it's a problem. I don't want some guy following me. It's creepy."

"I'll handle it." He held out a card to me. "Why is

she sending a card?"

"Who?" I took it and looked at the address label on the back. *Sylvia Barry.* "These came to the funeral home. She must have seen the death notice."

"Lightly said she reads the paper, remember? What does she have to say?" He sipped his drink, watching me speculatively.

I set down my drink and opened the envelope. A simple condolence card was inside. *Those we love are never gone. They live in our hearts forever.* Inside she wrote, *I'm sorry to hear of your mother's passing and sorry I'll be unable to attend her service. My sincere condolences on your loss.* It was signed with a tidy and precise *S Barry.*

Bell examined the envelope. "Los Olivos, California," he murmured. "I've heard of that. I think it's in the mountains, north of Santa Barbara. I wonder why she lives there."

"Maybe it's cheap," I said.

Bell snorted. "No place in California is cheap."

I sipped my drink and unfolded the list of people who requested to talk at the service. One person was from Mom's bridge club and another was the head librarian in town. "Do you want to talk at Mom's funeral?" I asked Bell, tossing the paper on the sideboard next to the cards.

"Do I need to reserve a spot?"

"Not really. I think the funeral director just wants to know how long a service to plan for. I expect he and the minister time it out."

"Yes, I want to talk. I'll give him a call and tell him." Bell stared into his drink, swirling the amber liquid around in the glass. "I wasn't able to be here when your father died."

"Where were you?" I asked, trying to sound casual. "I was surprised when you didn't show up for it. I mean, granted, we had broken up just a year or two earlier, but—"

"Two years, to be exact," Bell corrected. "We broke up when I was twenty-one and you were nineteen. I wanted you to run off with me and you wouldn't."

"I don't exactly remember it that way. As I recall, you wanted to drop out of school and hitchhike around Europe."

"Yep."

I shook my head. "Did you do it?"

He sipped his drink, leading the way out of the dining room and into the living room. Athos yawned and stretched elaborately, then jumped down and left the room, obviously uninterested in our conversation. Bell took a seat on the couch, avoiding Athos' well-furred spot.

"After I quit school, I bounced around the country for a while then I did go overseas. That's why I couldn't be here when your dad died. I didn't even know about it until I heard about your brother, Mike, dying. I called Dibs when I got back in the States to get caught up on people—you—and he told me about it."

"I read about your trip in Europe," I said, taking Mom's favorite chair. "*Time* had that article about you."

Bell smiled wryly. "It glossed over some of my more interesting adventures, like landing in a Swiss jail for almost a year."

I choked on my drink. Athos, who watched us

suspiciously, took that as an excuse to race out of the room. I would probably find him curled up on my bed later. "What?" I managed to croak.

"There's one other thing they've glossed over for all these years. I've made sure it doesn't get any air time in any stories about me." He walked across the room, staring down at the CD player. If he noticed his CD sitting on top, he didn't mention it. "It's something you need to know about me, Wendy. It's bound to come out sooner or later, and it's best that I tell you about it instead of you hearing about it from someone in the press who's done research on me."

I set my glass on a nearby end table and sat up straight in the chair, the picture of attention. "I'm ready, Mr. Bell. What big secret do you have to tell me? Let's see, you were in jail in Switzerland. Were you smuggling drugs?" I regarded him with mock seriousness. "No, I doubt that. You're too smart for that. Did you steal something? Maybe." I nodded thoughtfully. "I could see you doing that."

"This is serious, Wendy." He turned to face me, his face set and hard.

"I'm sure it is, Bell. And I'm sure I can find out all about it in the newspapers if I do a bit of digging."

"Not unless all my bribes are wasted." His pale green eyes searched my face as though he could find a clue to my feelings there.

His calm, unwavering stare was disconcerting. "What did you do, Bell? Don't tell me. You killed a man." I shook my head. "I doubt even the Swiss would forgive that."

He nodded. "You're right. It took me a while to convince them that it was justifiable homicide."

Chapter 9

"What?" I would have shot to my feet but I was so surprised I was literally paralyzed.

"I killed someone. There's something else you need to know." He sat down on the couch on my left and set his glass next to mine on the end table. "I have a daughter."

I stared at him, my jaw sagging. "What?"

He nodded. "She's not my daughter by blood, but I'm responsible for her. Her mother and I were involved. Filette was just a toddler when I met her mother. That's the nickname I gave her. Her real name is Fay." Bell stared down at the floor, his shoulders hunched. "Filette is handicapped. She's severely autistic. Her mother, Charmine, was a French student and she did drugs. Filette's father was an addict and— well, you can see where I'm going with this. I met Charmine when she was in Switzerland at a clinic, getting straight."

I managed to swallow around the lump in my throat. "Were you a patient, too?"

"No." Bell clasped and unclasped his hands, dangling between his knees. "I worked there. I bummed around a lot after college, getting odd jobs here and there. I went overseas and hitchhiked around Europe."

He smiled and I smiled tremulously in return. That was something he always wanted to do and something I could never imagine doing. It was one of the main reasons we broke up. Bell was always willing to lean over the cliff and see what was below. I always hung back.

"I was a guard on the premises. When Charmine was admitted, there was nowhere else for Filette to go, so they let her stay at the clinic. A mother-daughter deal, I guess you could say." He smiled coldly. "Charmine's parents were very high society and very wealthy and all they wanted was for their daughter and their illegitimate granddaughter to be out of sight and out of mind."

"How old were you?" My hand was shaking so hard it was difficult to pick up my glass. I managed, though, and drank down a lot of liquor, trying to still my thudding heart and slow down my racing brain.

"Twenty-four. Anyway, long story short— Charmine's boyfriend came looking for her at the clinic, we fought, and I killed him. It was an accident, but it took a while for the Swiss legal system to come to the conclusion that the world was better off with him dead. I was released, Charmine's parents took her away, and Filette was thrown into a mental institution and got no help whatsoever."

"What happened after that?" I probably didn't need to ask. I knew what Bell would do.

"Charmine died a year later of a drug overdose. Her parents wanted nothing to do with their grandchild, so I assumed responsibility for her and eventually formally adopted her. I got her into a good school in England and she learned some social skills. She can't live alone outside the group home, but she's okay where she is. She's twenty-six now." He frowned thoughtfully. "She's older than I was when I adopted her. Man, time sure does fly."

I could easily visualize Bell at that age, adopting a three-year-old child. He was such a free spirit in many ways, but he also had a strong sense of right and wrong. He would never abandon any vulnerable creature if he could do anything to help.

"I wanted you to know, because it might come out. My visits to her are strictly confidential and everything is paid through a third party, but the press can be dogged about that kind of thing. Every now and then Charmine's family makes a fuss and tries to shake me down for money by threatening to go to the press, but I have legal teams in Europe who handle them."

I thought about what he said while I took a sip of my drink. "Did my mother know?"

"Yes. I told her about it. We talked about your father and his death. I told her why I couldn't be here."

"Because you were in jail," I murmured. "Pretty good reason."

"I didn't want to just send a card or write a letter. It was years later before I found out. Your father died, your brothers died—" Bell looked at me, his face tight with sadness. "There are no words of sympathy for losses like that. I wish I could have been here. I would do anything I could to help, you know that."

I smiled. "I know. And I'm sure that Mom knew, too."

"I should have been here." He looked down at his hands, frowning. "I wanted to be here."

"Is that why you're so anxious to be with me again? Are you making up for your absence?" Before he could answer, I hurried on. "You don't owe us anything."

"It's not a matter of what I owe you." He raised his head to regard me. "You're family, Wendy. It's that simple."

Footsteps scuffled at the front steps and someone knocked. "It's not that simple. You and I have a complicated past." I reached for the front door.

"It's not complicated if we have a future," he said quietly.

I peered through the side window and opened the door. "We'll discuss this later."

He smiled. "I look forward to it."

Lightly and Totts entered, Totts carrying a twelve-pack of beer and Lightly a bottle of wine. "We weren't sure what was needed so we thought we'd cover the bases," Lightly said with a laugh, handing me the bottle.

"Dibs is right behind us. He's bringing the bourbon." Totts entered the room and held out his hand to Bell. "It's been a long time, Tom."

"How's it going, Totts?" Bell stood, shaking hands with the taller man. Seeing all of them together made me remember that they all played high school sports together and were in various male clubs together. They each had a set of memories in addition to the ones I had with them.

Dibs came shortly after that and soon we were all crowded into the dining room, drinks in hand, while Bell presided in the kitchen and babied his masterpieces in and out of the oven while we talked and drank. He set them on the counter with a flourish. "The world's best pizza," he said triumphantly.

"I get dibs on first piece," Dibs said and we all

laughed. We each filled our plates and went back into the dining room.

"I expect to see Nanna come over to me and wait for pizza crust," Lightly said. "She loved pizza. What kind of dog was she?"

"Big," Totts said around a mouthful of pizza. "She was like a small horse."

"Part Newfoundland and part Lab, I think." It seemed natural for Bell's leg to press against mine under the table. "She died about a year after Mike died. I think she had a broken heart. Mike and Dad were her favorites and they died within a couple of years of each other."

"That was tough for you and your mom," Dibs said. "First your father died then Mike had that swimming accident at college and drowned."

"And then Bell and I broke up and Bell went away then I went away and John went to the Army and suddenly the house was empty." I sipped my wine. "It was toughest on Mom, I think. She was so used to having kids running in and out."

"When did John join the Army?" Lightly asked.

"He went to college for a year but his heart wasn't in it. Then he took some odd jobs, but didn't find anything he liked. I think he always wanted to be a soldier. Finally, Mom told him to go if that's what he wanted so bad." I took another swallow of wine, my old griefs mingling with my new one. "Then he died, too, and Mom and I were left with each other."

There was a short, poignant silence at the table then Totts said, "I always enjoyed talking with your mom. She would stop in once a year to go over her legal affairs and she always talked about what you two were doing."

"Us two?" I asked, my hand pausing as I raised my glass.

"You and Tom. She and Tom were always in contact." Totts looked at Bell, puzzled.

"I wrote to her now and then," Bell said, his voice neutral and off-handed.

Now and then? I made a mental note to go through Mom's things one more time and see if I could find any of his letters.

"I would chat with her when she came into the bank," Lightly said, unaware of my simmering curiosity. "I remember one time around Christmas we were talking about exchanging Christmas cards and she was sorry to see that tradition not being done much anymore. She said it was often the only way to stay caught up with people. I told her about exchanging Christmas cards with Peter's mom and she was surprised I stayed in touch with her." Lightly shrugged. "Sylvia stayed in touch with me, really, not the other way around."

"I don't do many Christmas cards," I said. "There's not much to talk about, I guess."

"There'll be stuff to talk about this year," Dibs said with a sly smile at me and Bell.

I started to protest but Bell spoke first. "Where is Sylvia living? The last I heard, she was in California."

Lightly nodded. "Her card last year had a new return address on it. I noticed it because it was one of those labels that says, *I've moved*, or something like that. I got the card at the bank and I remember showing it to your mother, Wendy. I thought that was a good way to do two things at once—notify people about a change of address and send out cards."

"Tina lived in California, too," Totts said. "She moved out there after graduation. You remember her? Tina Lilly, Peter's girlfriend."

I nodded. "He always called her Tiger."

Lightly laughed. "He said she was a real tiger in bed. I don't know if I believe that or not, though. Seems to me they were more friends than, you know, girlfriend/boyfriend."

"Yeah." Dibs took another slice of pizza, his third. Totts looked like he wanted another slice, but he eyed Dibs' girth and restrained himself. "She died out in California a couple of years after she moved there. That was odd."

"Why was it odd?" I sipped my drink, watching the interplay between the four men. In some ways, it was like they had never been apart, but it was weird to see them as grown-ups when I had known them as young men. It was hard to separate memory from reality sometimes.

"She was swimming in the ocean, I think, near Santa Barbara." Dibs wiped his chin with his napkin before continuing. "High tide came in and she got caught in a cave or something like that. Tina was the strongest swimmer on the swim team. Why didn't she just swim out of there? Besides, what was she doing there in the first place?"

"The cove?"

"California," Dibs said with a sweeping gesture. "She was going to school at Ames, studying social work or something. She wanted to work on the Indian reservation over in Tama. Her father was part-Indian, remember? Anyway, she was in school and then she up and quits and moves to California. And two years after that she was dead." He shook his head. "Weird."

I glanced at Bell and saw the wheels churning in his mind. I could tell his detective would be called soon for another check into the past.

"Your mom never liked Tina," Lightly said. "Of course, I don't think she liked Peter very much, either."

"Mom never pulled punches about her opinions," I admitted. "Although she always did so in such a ladylike way."

An awkward silence fell then Bell said, "It's good you lived so nearby. You could visit her often."

I nodded. That was one reason I didn't move far away. The other reason was that I just wasn't that adventurous and had no desire to explore life away from Iowa. Des Moines was about as far away as I cared to go. Plus, after my brothers and father died, I knew Mom appreciated the fact I could come to be with her at all holidays and often in between. "It's weird to think I won't be visiting her anymore," I said softly. "I used to come and stay at least once a month, sometimes more often, especially after she got sick."

"Lots of adjustments to make," Bell murmured.

"If what they say in the newspapers is true, there are more adjustments than that in store," Totts said with another sly look.

"Don't believe everything you read." I glanced at Bell and saw his wide-eyed innocent look. I nudged him, hard, and he wiped the look off his face.

"One story said something about Shadow. It said you were looking for him. What's that about? Peter's dead isn't he?" Dibs took another slice of pizza. Totts gave in and took another one, too. I smiled at his capitulation.

Bell got up and made himself another drink, his back to the others in the room. "Is he? Or is there something about that night that no one ever knew about?"

I looked around the table. Lightly and Totts looked embarrassed. Dibs wouldn't look at me. "What?" I demanded. "You guys all look guilty. What happened?"

"Nothing," Dibs said quickly.

I shot him an admonishing look. "Dibs, you never did lie very well. What happened?" I looked at Bell when he sat back down, but he just shrugged.

Lightly and Totts exchanged a look. "It was a joke gone sour, I guess you could say," Totts said. He took a big bite of pizza, which effectively shut him up when the others darted cautionary looks at him.

"What joke?" I looked from one to the other. Lightly, Totts, and Dibs all looked uncomfortable. I recognized that look. They were hiding something. "What?"

"You know what a prankster Peter was," Dibs said after a long pause. "He was going to play a joke on everybody. He wanted to scare people and pretend to jump out that window."

"He did jump," I stated. "I saw him."

"Well, yeah, but—we caught him," Lightly said. "What?"

All three men starting talking at once.

"He said it would be a big joke on his mom."

"You know how she was never there."

"He said for once he'd be the one who ran away from home and he'd make her act like the grown-up for a change."

"I think it was payback. You know his mom slept around. Somebody told us she was sleeping with our guidance counselor, Jamie Lim."

"What?" I managed to interrupt the flow of words. "I thought Lim and Peter were—"

Bell nudged me. "What happened? How did you do it?"

Lightly, Totts, and Dibs exchanged a sheepish look. It was Totts who explained. "Remember fire safety drills in high school?"

I nodded. "We had to evacuate the building and stand around outside. They did them once a month or so, didn't they?"

Lightly took up the story. "Well, some of us guys were called on as junior Fire Marshalls. We were shown how to use a tarp to catch people who jumped. We used one of those life-net things. The fire department guys told us to use it as a last resort." He grinned but it faded when he saw Bell's frown. "I guess the fire department didn't use it much."

"They've got trucks and ladders and stuff," Dibs said. "They don't need tarps."

"Anyway," Lightly resumed, "we took the net thing out of the school locker room."

"I had a key," Totts said. "They stored it in the equipment locker."

"Peter told us to be ready at nine-thirty that night," Lightly said. "It would be dark enough by then on that side of the barn."

I tried to visualize the scene but I've never been good at directions. Bell knew immediately what they meant, though. "The barn was on an east-west axis," he said. "The doors and the window on that side faced

119

east."

Totts nodded. "It was northeast, I think. Anyway, it was in the shadows, away from the sunset. Peter used the side away from the house, the side that faced the fields. We were there, waiting for him, when he jumped. He hit the net and took off running."

"Did Sylvia know?" Bell asked. He was tense beside me, no longer loose and relaxed. I could tell his mind was racing a million miles an hour, trying to process all this information. I was beyond such activity. I was stunned.

The three men exchanged another puzzled look. "I don't think so," Totts said. "If she knew, she would never have identified that body. She thought Peter was dead."

"We expected him to show up on Monday at school and laugh about it," Dibs said. "That was the plan anyway."

"He said how he was going to make this dramatic entrance. Everybody would be out looking for him and he'd come to school, back from the dead." Lightly took a swallow of beer then belched softly. "Peter always was kind of a showoff."

"Then you and Tom were in that accident and"— Totts glanced at the other two men—"we kind of forgot about Peter. I mean, he didn't show up and I guess we figured maybe he really did run away."

"We weren't sure what to do," Dibs said. "We didn't want to get Peter in trouble."

And you didn't want to get yourselves in trouble either, I thought but didn't say.

"But a body washed up and his mother identified him," Bell said softly. "She thought he was dead."

"We all did," Lightly said. "That's why we never told anybody. We were afraid that the fall screwed him up and he stumbled away and drowned."

"We were worried about you, too. We thought you might be blamed. After all, you were so mad at Peter. We were afraid the police might think you were involved," Totts threw in.

"It was an accident," Dibs said. He was so anxious to talk his slice of pizza sat on his plate, forgotten. "Lim helped us cover it up. He was worried, too. It was his house. I suppose he was afraid the cops would charge him or something."

"He's lucky they didn't," Bell said. "As it was, he lost his job. I suppose everybody wanted to cover it up."

"Peter convinced us he had it all figured out," Lightly said hurriedly. "You know how he was, Tom. He was a math genius. He had all the probabilities figured."

"Not math, really." Bell swished the liquor around in his glass, idly watching it spin. "He was great at predictive analysis."

I looked at the others and was relieved to see they looked as confused as me. "What?"

"Peter could analyze the behavior of a game player and predict the moves the player would make. He couldn't predict the game itself, but he could usually predict how people would react to the games. Your father figured it out, Wendy."

Lightly leaned back in his chair. "That jerk. Is that why he always beat me when we played video games? He always had a fat bet on the game and he almost always beat me."

"And I'll bet he beat you only when he had a fat bet," Bell said. "He analyzed your style of play and he knew how the games worked. He could predict the effect your moves would have. Keep in mind the video games were primitive then. It was easy for somebody who could do that."

"He didn't always beat you," Dibs pointed out.

"That's because I knew what he was doing so I made sure I never acted predictably." Bell took another swallow of his drink, crunching down on one of his watered-down ice cubes. "All you had to do was pay attention to what you were doing when you played. It was easy to throw in a few moves that didn't make sense."

"I remember," I said, his words triggering a faint memory. "Dad talked about it. He said most games were set up to train people to make certain moves, to back them into corners."

"Exactly. That's why my app did so well," Bell said with a grin. "I based it on you and you were so predictable. It was up to the user to make you unpredictable."

"You rat." I nudged him and he shied away.

"Ticklish, remember?"

"Oh, I remember," I said warningly. "You may be unpredictable about some things, but you aren't about that."

"And Wendy," Totts pointed out. "You were always predictable about her."

Bell stared at him blankly.

"You were," Totts said defensively. "We all knew how you felt about Wendy."

Bell nodded, his eyes distant as though he was

looking at a memory. "Of course. The car accident."

"What?" Now it was Totts' turn to be confused.

Bell turned to me. "Peter knew I'd come after you. He rigged my car. He tried to kill us."

Chapter 10

We all stared at Bell. It was Lightly who spoke first. "That's crazy."

"Peter wouldn't have done that," Dibs said. I could tell he had recovered his composure because he was eating again. "How could he?"

"It would be easy. My car was in the parking lot at high school. I suppose I went in to shower after baseball practice. I always did."

"But he can't just drop to the ground and fiddle with the underside of your car in the parking lot," Totts pointed out. "There would be people all round there."

"But he could pop the hood and mess with something inside," Bell said grimly. "All you'd have to do on those old cars is reach in and pull out something. Don't forget, Peter and I worked on that car together. He was a top-notch mechanic. It would be easy for him."

"But you drove it," Totts objected. "It started and drove fine. What did the cops say caused the accident?"

"A tire blew and we went into the ditch. I couldn't control it." Bell's hand tightened on his glass.

I touched his arm. "It wasn't your fault."

"I never could figure that," Dibs said, finally pushing away his plate. "You took great care of that car, Tom. It was like your baby. How could you blow a tire?"

"Ran over something in the road?" Lightly asked.

"All it would take is a screw in the back tire," Dibs said, leaning back in his chair with a contented sigh. "You were on a gravel road filled with potholes. You hit one of those, and that would do it."

"That's still not saying somebody caused the accident," Totts, ever the lawyer, said. "There's a lot of ways you could just have an accident."

"It was a convenient one," Bell said. "You said it yourself. Everybody was worried about us. People forgot about Peter until a week or so later, when that body washed up. Or at least they didn't worry about him right away."

"And by then the trail was cold and he was long gone," I said softly.

Totts shook his head. "No way. Peter didn't run away. He got disoriented or something, he fell in the river, and he drowned. The police tracked his footsteps all the way to the river."

"But—" I looked at Bell, expecting him to refute it. Instead he just shrugged.

"There's no way to tell now, is there?" he said. "The authorities did the official ID from the dental charts and that was that." He chomped on another bit of ice from his glass.

"Then what was that you told a reporter about looking for Shadow?" Lightly regarded Bell warily. "Sounded like you thought he was still alive."

"Nah. I had to give them some story about why I was here besides the funeral. Otherwise the reporters would be bugging Wendy and trying to crash the service."

It sounded plausible to me and it must have

sounded okay to them, too, because the subject was dropped. Talk turned to getting caught up on what had happened since graduation and that kept us busy until almost ten o'clock when Dibs was the first one to push away from the table. "I've got a half-hour drive and I'd better do it before I'm too relaxed."

He rose and the others followed. "I'll be there on Friday, Wendy," Totts said, touching my arm in consolation. "Your mother was a special lady."

"I'm planning on it, too," Lightly said.

"Me, too," Dibs chimed in when we all moved toward the front door. "Are you going to be around for a while after the funeral?"

"I think so," I said. "I need to wrap up a few things, figure out what to do with the house. I took some vacation time on top of my bereavement leave, so I don't plan to go back to the office for another couple of weeks. I'm playing it all by ear." It wasn't until I spoke the words that I realized, somewhere in the back of my mind, was the idea that maybe I wouldn't go back at all. Work and my life in Des Moines seemed more than just a two-hour drive away. It felt like it was on another planet.

Totts shot me a questioning look, but lawyerly discretion prevailed. "We'll make sure to get together before you leave town," he said, kissing me on the cheek. "It was good to see you, Tom. Don't be a stranger when you come back to town to visit."

"Maybe he won't be coming back now that Mrs. Davis is gone," Lightly said, opening the door and stepping onto the stoop.

"Oh, I think I'll be around." Bell didn't look at me when he said it, but the others all exchanged knowing looks.

I moved outside with them, peering to the right through the misty fog. The dark sedan was gone. "I guess our eavesdropper got tired of watching the house," I said to Bell while I waved good-bye to the Lost Boys, hurrying to their cars parked in front.

"That bugs me." Bell closed the door behind me and walked back to the dining room, going to the window to look out. "The other guys don't know this one. I'm not top-drawer news, so why would a service send somebody else out here? I need to talk to that guy tomorrow and see who he's working for."

I cleared off the table and stacked the dishes into the dishwasher. "Maybe it's somebody new trying to break into the business."

"I can think of better ways to do that than to follow a middle-aged business executive around a small Midwestern town."

He sounded grumpy. No, he sounded depressed. That wasn't like Bell. I turned to look at him. He was still at the window, but he wasn't looking outside. He was staring down at the pictures in the china cabinet. Mom always said her china wasn't worth displaying, but her family was, so she carefully arranged the photographs between the wooden panels holding the glass panes in the top of the cabinet.

"What's wrong?" I asked, joining him.

He opened the cabinet door and took out a picture of our family from when I was just a child. I sat squeezed between David and John. Mike sat on my lap and I had my arms firmly around him to keep him from squirming. Mom and Dad stood behind us, laughing while we kids all looked solemn and serious. "This is such a good picture. Your parents really were great people. They were such good role models."

I moved to stand next to him. "I think they enjoyed having kids. I think a lot of people nowadays have kids because they think they should, but they don't really enjoy it. You know what I mean—those people who have kids booked into every possible sport, so busy they don't have time to really interact with the kid."

Bell put the photo back in its place and took out another, this one a high school graduation picture of me in my cap and gown. My thick, light brown hair was shoulder-length and cut into layers, all curled and styled on those god-awful hot rollers. Our school colors were dark green and gold. I was brandishing the dark gold mortarboard hat and my diploma and I had a broad grin, as though relieved and amazed that I had really graduated.

"You were so beautiful," he whispered, touching the woman-girl in the photo. "You still are, but in a different way." He said it almost absently, as though unaware I was even there. I think maybe he was talking to himself. "You were everything I wanted in life. I loved you so much. Life was perfect."

"You wanted travel and adventure, too. Don't forget that." I took the photo from him and put it back. "I couldn't do that. I'm not made for uncertainty."

"I know." He looked deep into my eyes and I saw that yes, he really did understand, finally. "It took me a long time to realize that it didn't mean you were a coward or weren't brave. That's what I thought at first. I think it made me feel better because you wouldn't go away with me. You were just an old stick-in-the-mud. Poor Wendy, tied to the earth, not able to fly away with me."

I smiled. "I didn't want that. I would never have enjoyed it."

"I know." He took my hand and pressed my palm against his cheek. His beard was stubbly against my skin. "I'm done running around, looking for happiness. I'm ready to admit that it's not a crime to want to stay in one place."

I caressed his face, gently brushing back a strand of his thick hair. "That's a good lesson to learn. It's important to know not only where you belong, but to know where you want to be."

"I want to be with you." He pulled me into his arms and I went willingly. It felt so right to be with him, to feel his body against mine.

His kiss was right, too. We started out tentative and hesitant, but we quickly moved to passion. It wasn't that he felt familiar. His body, and mine, had changed too much for that. But there was a sense of homecoming, a sense of safety that I would never have felt with a new man. He knew me and he accepted me. There would be none of the usual games that people played when they met and—

Fell in love? We broke apart. Bell laughed softly and looked to his left. "Nothing like being two silhouettes on the shade."

I followed his gaze and saw the window, which had the shades partially down. "No kidding."

He touched my face. "I'd like to stay."

"You can't. You drove here. If your truck is here all night that will give the reporters a real story to write about."

"Damn it." He sighed. "You're right."

It was now or never. I could stay on my safe path, going about my normal, everyday life. Or I could take a chance, jump on the carousel, and fly away with Bell.

"Of course, I don't care about that and neither do you. So why don't you stay?"

His eyes widened. "Are you sure?"

"If you keep asking questions, I might change my mind."

He quit asking questions.

****

It was the most natural thing in the world to wake up the next morning and have Bell in bed with me. It took a second to realize that we were in my room, in the home where I was raised, in the double bed that was mine throughout my growing up.

We used to wake up together in the cramped bed in the equally cramped bedroom in the apartment he shared with three other guys at college. And of course, before that in high school, we never had a night together. Our moments were stolen wherever we could find them.

I opened my eyes and found Bell regarding me from inches away. Athos was at the foot of the bed, pressed against Bell's legs. "You made a friend," I said. "He hasn't slept with me before this."

"I used to bring him treats when I visited your mom. He remembers me." Bell leaned closer and kissed the tip of my nose. "Thanks for letting me stay."

I brushed a kiss across his lips. "Thanks for wanting to stay." I glanced at the clock. "Time to get up and get this day going, I think."

"What's your hurry?" He scooted closer and drew me into his arms. Athos took the hint and jumped off the bed.

I barely heard him leave.

An hour or so later, Bell and I had showered and were tackling a plate of eggs and bacon in the dining room. "What's on your agenda for today?" he asked, sipping coffee. Athos was on the floor nearby, eyeing him hopefully. Bell crumbled some bacon and lowered it to the floor. Athos wandered near it, apparently disinterested until Bell switched his attention to me. Then the cat jumped on the meat and devoured it in an instant.

I smiled at their interplay, something obviously familiar to them both. "Nothing, really," I answered. "The cousins begin arriving this afternoon. We'll have dinner with Aunt Jane tonight. She has it set at the assisted living place where she lives. They cater special events and have a private dining room."

"Does that mean if I want time on your schedule, I'd better book it now?"

"The next few days will be hectic. Family today and tomorrow, of course. Most of the cousins will leave on Saturday, but a couple of them are staying to Sunday."

"Hmm." He reached over and took my hand. "Will you drive out to Jamie Lim's old farm with me today? I called the realtor and he said he'd leave it open for me to walk through." Bell grinned. "I guess they aren't too worried about break-ins."

I squeezed his hand. "I'll go with you, sure, if we can do it this morning." I glanced at the window where sunlight was streaming in. "At least it finally quit raining so we won't have to slosh through too much mud if we walk around."

"You sound pessimistic."

"I'm realistic," I corrected. "Trust me." I looked under the table at his footwear and saw Athos leaning against his leg. "Your sneakers might get a bit mucky."

Bell gave Athos another bite of bacon then straightened. "You realize if I leave here wearing the same clothes I wore last night the reporters will have a field day."

I frowned, feeling a moment's panic at the thought. Then I decided, hell, what did it matter what anybody thought of me? I didn't live in town, anyone who knew me knew that Bell and I were old friends, and I wasn't really worried about my so-called reputation.

"I've got a jacket you can wear," I said after a moment's consideration. "Nobody will notice if you're wearing the same jeans as last night."

"Good idea. Maybe I need to pack a bag if we're going to do this again." He waggled his eyebrows at me.

"Or maybe I should and we can stay in your penthouse." I waggled my eyebrows right back at him.

He grinned. "I'm sure we can work out something."

"Well, we're not going to work out anything for a few days, until the family comes and goes. Let's cross that bridge when we need to." I looked at the rooster-shaped clock over the kitchen sink. "It's ten now. Let's go out to the farm and look around. I want to go through those notebooks of Dad's, too. Are they at the hotel?"

"They're at my penthouse, yes." He grinned at me. "I skimmed through them yesterday."

"I got these from Mom's jewelry box." I went to

the sack I brought home from the bank and pulled out the papers I jammed inside. "Mom left me this note. Aunt Jane said that Dad saw Peter the night he disappeared. He talked to Sylvia about it, but she just blamed you and me for what happened."

"God forbid Sylvia should blame Peter," Bell muttered. He sorted through the pages, frowning. "Copies of specific pages from your dad's journals. I wonder why?"

"Did you see anything in the journals about Peter?"

"Your father had random notes about a lot of us— Totts, Peter, me, you, your brothers. I'll go back and look at them closer. And he had pieces of software code he worked on." Bell looked off into space then said, "There was one entry that caught my eye. I need to re-read it."

"*We* need to re-read it," I corrected. "Maybe I'll see something you missed."

"You're convinced now, aren't you? You think Peter is alive, too."

"I'm keeping an open mind. Oh. That reminds me." I fished into the sack and pulled out the slip of paper from Aunt Jane with her loopy writing on it. "Jane told me to give you this. When I mentioned that you thought something was fishy with Mom's heart attack, she jumped on the idea. She said she did some research."

Bell stared at the paper, frowning while he tried to puzzle out the word. "What's that letter?" He held it out to me.

"I think it's a c. Or maybe it's an a. It's hard to tell."

A look of dawning understanding came over his face, reminding me of the old days when he would be working on a software program and then—bang—he had it debugged. "It's cocaine." He pulled out his phone and started typing.

"What?" I took the piece of paper and stared at it. I suppose it did sort of look like *cocaine* if you squinted just right.

"Cocaine. There were stroke victims at the hospital where I worked. They were coke addicts. It could cause strokes or"—he stared down at the phone screen—"it can cause a heart attack even in a healthy person. Your mother had cardiac problems, didn't she?"

I nodded. "Arrhythmia," I said. "She took medication for it."

"This article says that cocaine can cause arrhythmia and can constrict blood vessels to the brain." He tapped his phone.

"Stroke." My mind was spinning, sorting through everything mentioned in the last few days. "Someone was with her right before her heart attack."

Bell looked up from his phone, his face taut with anger. "Someone could volunteer to get her a glass of water, or a cup of tea. If they brought cocaine that was already dissolved, they could drop it into a drink and a few minutes later, your mother—" He took a deep breath.

"But why? I keep coming back to that. Why? After all this time, why now? Why my mother? Why would someone come after her in February?"

"I don't know." Bell shook his head slowly, his tousled hair falling forward onto his forehead. "Something precipitated it. Maybe there's something in the notebooks. We need to look at those as soon as we can."

"Then let's get going." I stood and took my plate and his to the kitchen. Bell followed with our coffee mugs and silverware. We stacked everything into the dishwasher then headed for the back door.

"Wait a minute." I went back to the living room and grabbed the CD from the stack on the player. I gave Athos a quick pat, interrupting his cleaning ritual. He shot me a dirty look and I could almost hear his sigh of exasperation when he reapplied himself to cleaning the spot I just touched.

"I want to hear this," I said, brandishing the CD.

"What—oh. You found that."

"Yep, I did." I took a sweatshirt jacket from a hook. "Here." I tossed it to Bell and he pulled it on, covering his pale blue denim shirt. I took a red sweater, pulling it on over my red-and-blue blouse. We stepped out of the house—

—and six people rushed us all at once. I took a step back but Bell kept his hand on my shoulder, propelling me forward. "Guys, I thought we had a deal," he said, slipping ahead of me and barreling through the men who surged forward. He held up his key fob and the truck made chirpy noises.

"Bets are off, T.K.," one said. "Stories are popping up about you all over. Somebody is dishing on you and we want in on it."

"Wendy, what's it like to be reunited with your first love?" someone shouted.

"Why do you think he was my first love?" I shot back.

Bell dragged us both to his truck and managed to get the passenger door open by leaning back and knocking into two reporters who were trying to photograph us.

"T.K., does this mean you're settling down?" someone else called.

Bell helped me up into the truck, almost shoving me onto the seat. I managed to collapse into the interior, tangling with a reporter outside who was trying to take pictures.

"If I am settling down, you'll be the last to know." Bell slammed my door and pushed his way through the crowd to the other side of the truck. He looked pissed off, his normally placid face taut with anger. He said something to one of the reporters from the previous day—Juko, I think his name was—and the man said something in return that made Bell glare at him.

Someone pulled open my door. "Wendy, do you plan to move to California or New York to be with T.K.?"

I grabbed the door, almost overbalancing and falling out. "None of your damn business." I pulled the door shut, nearly un-fingering someone in the process.

Bell slid into his seat. "Sorry about that," he muttered, tapping the keyless ignition. The engine roared to life and he started to back down the drive, apparently not worrying about the people still surrounding the truck. He reached the street and we took off with a screech of tires. I turned to look behind us and saw people racing for cars.

"They're following."

"They can try," he said through clenched teeth. He pushed the gas pedal to the floor.

Chapter 11

I've never been in a high-speed chase, but I imagine it was like that exhilarating ride on Gloucester Road, past the high school, then onto Highway 1 looping around town. Two cars followed behind us, far enough back that when Bell turned off onto a county two-lane blacktop and started zigzagging along farm roads, the cars quickly fell back. The recent rains kept our telltale dust to a minimum and within ten minutes we were free of pursuit.

"Good driving," I said admiringly. "You know your way around some back roads."

"I'm just glad they haven't changed since you and I used to come out here and neck," he said with a grin. "This is my stomping ground, remember?"

I laughed. "Some things a girl never forgets." I fumbled for the CD I grabbed and slipped into the slot on his dashboard. "Do you remember how to get to the farm from here?"

Bell smiled. "Some things a boy never forgets." He reached up and cracked open the sun roof. "Let's enjoy the fresh air. I feel like it's been raining for a week."

We drove in companionable silence punctuated by the music playing on the CD. The farm fields that were recently planted were showing just the faintest haze of green. Other fields that would be planted later were still golden from last year's crop. Sun was shining through fat white clouds, the previous day's rain a thing of the past. Everything had a fresh, sparkling look. Even the ditches, most of them full of water, looked lush.

"I always forget how much I like this part of the country until I come back again," Bell said while he made the various turns that would take us back toward town but on the roads outside it. "When you're in a city you lose touch with the seasons or else your perception is shaped by inconvenience. You know—the roads aren't plowed or it's too hot to go outside or something like that."

I looked off into the distance. This part of the state had gently rolling hills, shallow dips and swells in the land. Pioneers settled this country in their "Prairie Schooners", which was an apt form of transportation for land that had the feel of the ocean. "I know what you mean. City people go to a park and feel they're surrounded by nature. It isn't until you're here"—and I gestured to the expanse of land in front of us—"that you understand how small we really are in the scheme of things."

"There are so many stars at night in the sky here." Bell stopped at a gravel road intersection and peered right then left. I didn't give any directions, but he glanced at me before turning right. "It's almost like being in the mountains. There's nothing like being on a county road at night and looking up and seeing the sky."

I knew exactly what he meant. He and I had done that many a time, driving to a deserted spot, climbing up on the roof of his car, and staring into the sky. Of course, those interludes often led to more adventures in the back seat of his car, too, but I would never forget those starry nights under a clear sky.

I stole little glances at Bell while he drove. In so many ways, he looked like the boy I used to know, but he had changed. He wore his hair the same, cut shorter around his ears and long on top, and there was gray around his temples now. His face was lined and rougher looking, but the same basic structure was there—the deep dimples at his cheeks when he smiled, the way his eyes crinkled up when he laughed, and the oval shape of his face ending in a slightly dimpled chin.

He was my memory but he wasn't, too. Last night was familiar and yet tantalizingly new. I felt no hesitation or worry about what he might think about my less-than-young body. I was still slender, thanks more to good genetics and my regular exercise program than to any diet. But I wasn't still firm and perky. I wasn't sixteen.

But I knew that didn't matter to him. I knew he saw me through the filter of our past just as I saw him that way. Bell had seen me at my best, when I was all prettied up for a date, and at my worst, when I drank too much and puked in a cornfield. The same was true with me. I had seen him so handsome it took my breath away, and so dirty and sweaty from working he looked like Pig Pen from the Charlie Brown cartoon strip.

Our loving last night wasn't the crazy impetuousness of youth but had the feeling of maturity where both adults realize that this is something to be treasured, not taken for granted. It made me feel appreciated. It made me feel loved.

"There it is."

I looked to the right at the two-story farmhouse set back from the road, its once-blue paint now faded to a pale gray. The trim around the windows looked somewhat white and the glass in the panes glittered in the fitful sunlight. "I'm amazed it's still standing. That house has to be at least sixty years old."

Behind the house the barn stood, or rather leaned. Its color had faded from bright red to a brownish-umber and even from this distance I saw light filtering through the cracks between the boards. It looked like a strong wind might take it down, although it appeared most of the wood was intact.

"They built them to last back in the day." Bell stopped the truck about halfway down the quarter-mile graveled farm lane. "Can't you imagine it?" He framed an imaginary view with his hands. "I'll put in big picture windows in front, so I can see the lane. Wouldn't that be great to have picture windows in an office? We'll plant trees there and there." He pointed to spots at the sides of the house, where bedraggled shrubs now squatted. "Then we'll add flowers in a big arc right in front. I want a fireplace, too. Maybe two."

I squinted at the vision he tried to present while he drove slowly forward. "That barn looks iffy."

"But maybe we can salvage the wood."

"Salvage it? For what?"

Bell shrugged, parking the truck in the rutted farmyard. "I don't know. It's so nicely aged."

"Make sure you check on the well and the septic. They're probably nicely aged, too."

"Huh?"

"There's probably a private well." I pointed to the old metal windmill behind the house, its turbine unmoving in the gentle breeze. "And a septic system," I explained patiently. "We're in the country, so they won't be on city water or sewer. Make sure that's okay before you go designing the house. Trust me. You don't want a faulty septic system, especially in the middle of summer."

He grinned. "That's my Wendy. Ever practical. That's why we make such a great team. You figure out all the little details and I go for the big picture."

"You wouldn't call it a little detail if your sewer backed up," I snapped. "Or if you got sick from e coli in the well."

"The big details," he amended. "Come on." He stepped out of the truck and started toward the house.

I got out and walked around the farm yard before following him to the rundown building. As with most farms, the gravel area between the house, the detached garage, and the barn was graded relatively smooth, with just a few deep potholes. It wasn't anything that a backhoe and a new load of gravel couldn't cure. The barn was to the east of the house, again a standard arrangement. Prevailing winds were usually out of the north or west and you don't want your barn smells invading your house, especially in summer.

I turned slowly in a circle, taking in the out-buildings. All in all, the property looked acceptable. It was weedy, but not overgrown. Whoever was leasing the fields probably mowed the area, at least now and then. A load of gravel, some structural work on the barn, and some paint and things would start to look okay.

I went in the side door of the house where Bell had disappeared. I entered a kitchen, sadly outdated and in need of a good scrubbing. The linoleum tile floor was still intact but scuffed badly. It was a black-and-white pattern, with smaller diamond tiles at the sides. The metal cabinetry used to be white, and was probably disgusting inside, but the walls and windows looked solid, with no signs of water intrusion.

Bell was nowhere in sight but I heard footsteps upstairs. I checked out the main floor which consisted of a living room, dining room, and a small "spare" room that probably used to be a TV room. The whole house had wood floors, scuffed but not warped. The dining room and living room had ugly wallpaper peeling in spots, but it also had beautiful oak woodwork, the kind you don't see anymore. It was hard to gauge the size of the rooms without furniture, but they all felt good sized.

Big windows let in the light and all of them were unbroken, which surprised me. The house was cool but not too musty, which I expected from a closed-up structure. I spied the thermostat on the wall. It was set at 50 degrees, which meant that enough heat had been kept on to keep the pipes from bursting during the winter. There was shade from the trees on the south side of the house, so it would probably stay somewhat cool in the summer.

I walked up the paint-chipped wooden staircase. Bell waited at the top. "I was right," he said. "It's in bad condition but it's fixable. Look, I can put an office up here. What a great view." He walked into the front room, which did indeed have a good view of the lane and the fields in the distance. It faced south and slightly west. If he took out the two small windows and put in one large one, it would be light-filled and feel more spacious.

He walked through the other three bedrooms,

talking about changing this and that. I followed, bemused by his enthusiasm. My ex-husband had been indifferent to color, furniture styles, or design, so seeing a man who was obviously so intrigued by design was a new experience for me. Of course, Bell was a designer. His app was proof of that. It would certainly be interesting to embark on a remodel project with someone who was not only enthused but someone who had an unlimited budget.

"The good thing is I can stay at the hotel—my penthouse, as you call it—while the construction is going on. Nothing worse than living in a house while it's being worked on." He stopped at the top of the stairs. "Maybe we can steal some space from the front room, expand the back bedroom and make it the master suite. How's that sound?"

I went down the stairs. "It sounds expensive." I went into the living room, turning to face him when he joined me. "You'll probably have to replace the plumbing and most of the electric."

"I suppose," he said absently. "I wonder about the barn."

"What about the barn?" I followed him through the kitchen and out the back door.

"I'd like to make a private place for Filette." He smiled tentatively at me. "Maybe she could come for a visit. She has a full-time nurse and I can rent a private plane for them. It might be okay for her."

"Let's go look." I didn't want to squash his optimism but I doubted that a severely autistic young woman could handle international travel, private nurse or not.

We walked into the farmyard and I pointed out

spots that would need re-grading. At this time of day, the barn blocked some sunlight and I was reminded of our talk with The Lost Boys. "The guys were right last night." I walked around to the far side of the structure. "There's the hay loft door. It faces east and it's away from the house."

Bell looked up at the doorway, which was closed, his eyes shifting from the ground to the second story then back again. "It would be an easy jump as long as somebody was there to catch you. If somebody wasn't, you'd probably break an ankle or at least get a sprain or bruised." He walked a few yards beyond the barn. "The river is about a half-mile through the field. If he had a flashlight, it would be an easy walk."

We walked around the perimeter of the barn, each of us deep in thought. Peter had deceived us, for all these years. For so long I had a nagging sense of guilt that I caused him to despair, that I was the cause of his depression. And there he was, living well on the life insurance money. The more I thought about it, the more pissed off I got.

"The barn needs a lot of work," Bell admitted.

"You know, it might be better than you think. You can get a barn restoration specialist. Somebody like that would be your best person to evaluate whether it's worth keeping or not."

We walked to the truck and Bell turned in a slow circle to regard the property. "I want to buy it." He stopped and looked at me. "What do you think?"

I drew in a deep breath of warm Iowa air, redolent with the smell of earth, grass, and life. "It's a good spot. Better than any apartment in some high-rise somewhere."

He grinned. "Spoken like a true farm girl." He got into the truck.

"I'm not a farm girl," I corrected, climbing in the passenger side.

"You're close enough to one to count. Do you have time for a drive?"

"Where to?" I buckled my seat belt and leaned back.

"I thought we could drive out to the lake. I'll show you the spot where your mom and I went to feed the pelicans."

I was speechless for an instant then I said, "Thank you. I'd like that a lot."

He squeezed my hand. "I loved her, too."

I looked out my window, tears slipping down my face. Tomorrow was the funeral. Loss seized me and I wasn't sure I could breathe, much less talk. "I miss her," I finally said.

"I know." It wasn't just a simple acknowledgement of how I felt. It was a statement about his grief. His sense of loss was as great as mine.

I blinked hard to stop the tears and glimpsed a road sign. "Three miles to the corner turnoff," I said.

"What?"

"The sign back there. It said it was eight miles to Kensington. The turnoff is five miles from town. That means we're three miles from the turnoff."

Bell shook his head. "It never fails to amaze me that you have no idea if we're going north or south but you always know where we are when we're outside of town."

"I'm just a farm girl," I said. "We always know our way around the country."

He laughed and was still chuckling when we got to the intersection for the lake. He turned right and in a few minutes, we were there. "Lake" was probably too grand a term for the large but somewhat shallow body of water that occupied several acres of land north of town. Several lakes like this dotted the landscape in the southern part of the state in declivities dug out by the glaciers that came through the area umpteen years ago.

Bell pulled into the park adjacent to the lake and took the curving, narrow drive around the perimeter. "We came here in the fall last year. That's when the birds migrate. They come through in early spring, too, but your mom was—she couldn't come and see them this spring. We saw them in other years, though."

She couldn't come and see them because she was lying partially paralyzed in a hospital bed, trapped in her body, fed in small bites and cared for by nurses around the clock. Once again tears rolled down my cheeks and this time I didn't care if he saw them or not. My mother had been a vibrant, active woman. Her manner of death was a travesty. It was even more of a travesty if someone caused it, as Bell suspected.

The thought chilled me. It was one thing to suppose Peter duped the authorities. It was another to accuse him of murder or attempted murder. Could he really have killed some poor homeless veteran and then returned to town to hurt my mother?

Even as I questioned it, I knew the answer. Of course he could. Peter had been chillingly amoral, like a child who doesn't know right or wrong, a child who cares only about *me*. Peter always saw the world in terms of what it could do for him or how it might affect him. Other people were obstacles or tools to be used.

He used his charm and his boundless energy to manipulate people to do what he wanted.

Bell pulled into a parking area on the eastern side of the lake, one of many small lots that could hold a dozen or so cars. There was no one else there today, but it was the middle of the week, so that wasn't surprising. "This was one of her favorite spots. It has a clear view all the way across the lake." He turned off the engine. "Do you want to go see?"

I was already opening my door. "Over there, by the picnic tables?" I thought I recognized it from the photographs on Mom's camera.

He joined me and we walked the few yards to the tables set on a grassy area not far from the lake's edge. The ground was spongy, not surprising given all the rain in the last few days, and it was a dark, glossy green. Beyond the grass was a rock-strewn bit of sandy beach, more for lounging than swimming. It all smelled clean and fresh, not pungent the way it would in middle summer when vegetation started to decay.

"We would sit on the picnic table and your mom would toss bread in the water. Pretty soon a bird would show up and then another." Bell sat on the bench of the table, turned so the surface was at his back. I sat next to him, staring at the lake and visualizing what he was saying. "It was funny. There was never a big flock of them, like there is when somebody feeds pigeons or geese. It was like the birds were being polite and not mobbing her."

I leaned back into the circle of his arm on the table behind me. Sunlight was warm on my face. I closed my eyes and could easily visualize my mother, her face flushed with cold and her dark blue eyes dancing with laughter when the birds came to her for their treats. "Never birds," I murmured. "A Never bird rescued Peter in the book."

Bell's arm tightened on my shoulders. "If we're right about Peter…" His voice trailed away.

"If we're right about Peter, I hope no one rescues him," I said flatly. I opened my eyes, returning to reality. "I need to go through the notebooks. There must be something in there from Dad. Something that will help us figure out what happened. Why did Mom copy pages that weren't pertinent?"

Bell was silent next to me. When he didn't answer, I looked at him. He had that faraway look I recognized, that *I'm in debugging mode and don't bother me* look. "What did your mother's note say?" he asked in an equally faraway voice.

"She said the papers rightfully belonged to me and she kept them secret because she wanted to spare me."

"She said *does a week or a month matter,* didn't she?"

I frowned, dredging up the memory of the note. "Yes, something like that, I think."

"That's it. That's the key. It's not the physical key, but it's the key to the notebooks."

I shook my head. "I don't get it."

"She copied certain pages. The really important pages will be a week or a month different than the dates on the pages she copied." He jumped up, pulling me to my feet. "Come on. There is something in those notebooks. We just have to find it."

I hurried after him while he raced back to the truck. We got inside and he drove as fast as the narrow park drive would allow to the main road, talking excitedly the entire time. "If I'm right, there must be something in the notebooks that can prove Peter was still alive even after Sylvia identified that body."

I caught a glimpse of movement in the rear-view mirror on my right. A blue pickup, old and rusty, puttered along behind us. It was the first car I'd seen since we entered the park except for a dark mini-van that followed us in. As we neared the exit, which was also the entrance, I saw the van still parked there.

Bell made a right turn at the main county road and headed back toward town, picking up speed on the two-lane blacktop road. "I bet the reporters are camped out at your house. I left the notebooks at the hotel. We should go there."

"Why don't you drop me at my house?" I suggested. "I'll talk to the reporters for a few minutes and that might give you enough time to slip away."

"Good plan. It might even work. If you can stall them—"

Crunching, grinding noise interrupted him. I was pushed forward, my seat belt keeping me from hitting the dash, but just barely. "What's going—?"

More crunching, crashing, and screeching as Bell slammed on the brakes. The truck continued forward, skewing on the road. It smelled terrible, the scent of burning rubber filling the cabin. "Damn it, the idiot behind us is hitting me. He's pushing us."

I tried to swivel on the seat to peer behind us, but another violent crash jerked my head so sharply I swore I heard a muscle pop. "What's he doing?"

Bell jerked the steering wheel sharply to the right and the rear of the SUV skidded toward the opposite side of the road. "Hold on," he shouted.

I grabbed the door strap with my right hand but didn't have time to grab anything else. The truck behind us slammed into the passenger side—my side—of the truck. I saw it coming and leaned as far away as I could. Bell let go of the wheel and threw himself over me.

The world turned upside down.

Chapter 12

It was a repeat of that accident long ago only this time it seemed to run in slow motion, as though it was a choreographed dance. Our truck slipped off the road and tumbled into a ditch. I think I screamed or maybe it was all in my head. I don't know if I would have even heard myself it I did.

The world was full of noise. Crunching, screeching, screaming metal, objects flying around the passenger cabin, Bell's steady cursing. I stiffened, waiting for the air bags to deploy but they didn't do a thing, a fact that barely registered amid the chaos. The car made noises, alarm sounds that dinged and buzzed and dinged again. Over all of it, the CD still played, Death Cab for Cutie singing *I Will Follow You into The Dark.* I fervently prayed that it wasn't a prediction of what would come.

I jerked and slammed into my seat belt, dangling there for seconds before the truck moved again, pushing me in another direction. I was vaguely aware of pain but mostly I was scared. I clung to Bell and it wasn't until I realized he was lying completely over me that I also realized he must have unhooked his seat belt. "Get back," I said, pushing at him. "You need to be strapped in—"

The truck lurched again, crashing into something immovable. We settled to a stop on our side, the driver's part of the SUV now underneath us and my door on top. An eerie silence drifted over us then the grinding sound of tortured metal was a prelude to another lurch, and another settling of the SUV. With a wheezing cough and shudder, the engine shut off and the dings and clicks shut off with it.

"Get out." Bell reached for my seat belt strap. "Get out, there's water."

"What?" I barely heard him. My ears buzzed and everything was blurry.

"Get out, Wendy. Come on, move." He fumbled underneath me for the seat belt closure and it sprang free. I almost fell on top of him, stopping myself by grabbing for the door. "Open your door. I can't do it from here. You need to open it. There's water coming in."

Water. I smelled it now. Ditch water, not stagnant but also not clean. Pungent and warm-smelling with dirt and grass mixed in. I twisted in the seat and touched my door handle, now above me. I pulled up on the handle and pushed as hard as I could. The door didn't budge. "That truck hit us on this side," I gasped in between pushes. "I think it's jammed. It won't move."

"Okay. You're right. It's probably too crushed." Bell sounded amazingly calm. I gave up on the car door and turned in the seat, putting a hand on the side of Bell's seat to keep me from falling on him. He lay against the driver's side window and was waist-deep in water, his legs completely covered. Blood dribbled down his face from a cut on his forehead and he clung to the steering wheel, using it to keep him away from the water filling that side of the car. "Go out the back. Climb over the seats and get the back hatch open."

"How deep is the water?" I managed to turn completely in my seat and wedge myself against the console, keeping me relatively stable. It was big enough to keep us separate if I didn't move too much. I peered into the back of the SUV which was lit by sunlight filtering into the interior through the sun roof. "There's water back there, too."

"There's water all along the driver's side. It's not coming in the sun roof but if the truck settles any more it might. See if you can climb over the seat. The headrest might be in the way, but you should be able to adjust it. If you can get over it, you can climb out the back."

"What about you? Can you break out the windshield or something?"

"I'm stuck. My foot got jammed when the truck went over. You'll have to get out and get help somehow."

I gaped at him. "I can't leave you here. Are you crazy?" I looked at the water, still around his waist but now slightly higher. "How deep is it?"

"This is a steep ditch. We've had a lot of rain." He smiled briefly but it was strained and I wondered what 'jammed' meant. Was his foot or ankle broken? "I doubt I'm going to drown but it's damn uncomfortable. See if you can get out."

I nodded. "Okay. I'll figure out something." No way was I leaving him, but maybe I could find a way to free him. I twisted and put my right foot against the dash to get some leverage, but stunning pain made me scream out and drop back onto the console, which now served as my seat. "Shit. I think my ankle is broken."

Bell used the steering wheel to twist himself. "Let

me see it."

I lay squished against the console, my ribs aching. It hurt to breathe deeply. "It's okay," I said, panting for breath. "I just need to be careful, that's all." Bell was counting on me. He was trapped and I wasn't. It didn't matter if my damn leg was broken. I had to get him out.

"Let me see it," he insisted.

"It's okay. Just let me try again." I used my arms to push against the console and I managed to wiggle until I was poised to attempt to scale the passenger seat. I tried to look around, but my neck was so stiff. If I turned it, crazy pain shot down my right arm.

"Hey!" A tapping sound came from somewhere.

I twisted, landing on my side and resting partially on Bell, caught between the two front seats. I looked to my right, to what used to be the SUV roof. Murphy Black, the reporter I met the previous day, was perched on the side of the SUV, peering over the edge of the roof and into the glass sunroof.

"Tom? Are you okay? We saw what happened." He shifted position and the truck shifted with him. "Oh, shit. Damn. Hold on."

"Where did they come from?" I asked Bell, who was just a few inches away, reclining against the driver's side of the car. The water was over his waist and inching up toward his chest. I tried not to panic when I saw that.

"They must have been following us." Bell sounded exhausted and he looked it, too.

"Are you okay? How's your foot? How bad are you hurt?" I touched his face, as much to comfort myself as him.

"I banged up my ribs and probably sprained my

ankle. How about you? How's your foot?" He tried to sit straighter, but grimaced and rested back again, the water creeping ever higher.

"I'm fine. Where are they? What are they doing?" I couldn't shift position because if I did, my ribs hurt like crazy. I cautiously raised my head and saw Billy Juko peering into the car.

"Hey, we called the police. They're on the way." He tried to smile but it looked forced.

"We need to get out now." I pointed downward. "There's water."

"What?"

"Water," I shouted. "We've got water."

Juko crept over the edge of the SUV, raised himself up on his hands, and looked downward. "Oh, fuck," he muttered. "Okay, hang on." He carefully inched off the SUV. "Murphy! We got trouble here!"

"No shit, we've got trouble." I eased away from Bell until I was resting half in the passenger side foot well and mostly on the console. "Let me see if I can get your foot out."

"I think it's under the brake." Bell straightened and his right leg moved. "I think the gas pedal came loose or something, and my foot is stuck behind it."

Like a contortionist, I folded up my body as much as I could until I was almost completely in the foot well. I peered around the gear shift, resting my chin on its knob. From that vantage, I could see into the driver's foot well, which was filled with muddy water.

Through a series of careful maneuvers, I managed to wiggle my right arm downward. The truck shifted again, just as I touched Bell's leg. "Careful," he said through clenched teeth.

I didn't have any spare breath to reply. I ran my hand down his blue jeans in the mucky water, finally reaching his ankle. I traced the outline of his foot, closing my eyes to try to visualize what was there. "You're right. Your foot is under the brake and it feels like something's on top. Can you twist it a bit?"

"I'm not sure. It might be broken."

I put my hand against the side of his foot and nudged it. "Okay?"

"Yeah, but it's not moving."

"We're going to break out the window." Juko tapped on the passenger side window above me. "The windshield is probably too tough to break. Cover your face, okay?"

I couldn't twist enough to see him. "Okay," I called back. I lowered my face, inches from the muddy water swirling around Bell's legs. I felt him shift and cover his face with his arm. As he did, I nudged his foot again, trying to explore in the cloudy water without disturbing him. There was enough room for him to move if—

"I'm going to take off your shoe," I said. "If we can get it off, your foot will slip past the brake pedal. Hang on." I scrabbled below me, unable to see anything, working by feel. I struggled with the laces, patiently picking at the loop.

"Hang on in there!"

I didn't dare try to turn. I was so tangled up with Bell that if I did, I was liable to tip him further into the water or tip myself.

"Get ready, Wendy. Keep your face down." Bell put his hand on the back of my neck, keeping me turned from the window above me.

A crunching, smattering sound echoed in the car. "What's happening?" I slipped my hand around the heel of his shoe, trying to slide it off his foot.

"They've got a tire iron. Hold on."

Another crunching, then another, then another. The SUV shuddered with each blow, each time tipping a little bit more and a little bit more. "Tell them to stop. We'll tip over then we'll be totally in the water." I tried to ease back, but Bell kept his hand on my neck.

"One more," he shouted. "It's almost out."

"Bell, they'll push us over completely if they—"

Smash! Glass fell around us, small rectangular chunks. At the same moment, Bell jerked, his shoe catching on the brake pedal. I felt it drift to the floor of the car when his leg came free. His momentum turned me and I almost went face-first into the muck. Then he caught me in his arms, pulling me against him.

"Get up there," he said. "Take your sweater and cover your hands. There might be glass in the opening." He kissed me quickly then pushed me away. I was wet along the right side of my body from lying in the water with him.

"I've got it handled." Murphy wiped out the glass edges from the window with what looked like a man's shirt, probably his own since it appeared he was wearing a yellow T-shirt. "Come on, Wendy. Let's get you out."

Bell pushed me upward and between him behind and Murphy above, I was dragged out of the window. I couldn't do much to help them because my right foot hurt to put any weight on it and my ribs were tender. I just bit my lip and did my best.

Murphy helped me slide off the SUV and Juko

caught me. He was on the side of the ditch, one leg in the mucky water and the other on the bank. He grabbed me with his left hand and with his right he held on to a rope that was in turn lashed to a road sign above us. I staggered to the bank, out of the water, and flopped down, waving him off. "Go help. Bell might be hurt. Help get him out."

I propped myself up on my elbows and watched Murphy lean into the SUV, legs dangling over the undercarriage. When I saw Bell's head emerge from the car, I flopped back on the grass. When I heard the sirens in the distance, I decided it was probably okay to pass out.

I wasn't out for long. When I opened my eyes, Bell lay on the grass next to me. He was wet up to his arm pits, his once blue shirt brown with mud and his jeans caked with it. When he saw me look at him, he rolled over carefully and put his left arm across my middle. "I was afraid I'd lose you," he whispered, his breath warm on my face. He leaned his face against mine.

"You're stuck with me, Bell." I turned my head and kissed him.

"I saw what happened," Murphy said, scrambling up the wet, grassy bank to kneel next to us. "We both saw it. That truck jammed you. They rammed you right into the ditch."

"I got the license plate number," Juko said. He stood on the road above us, waving his arms. "It was blue. I think it was a Ford."

"Chevy," Murphy said. "Don't move, you guys. The paramedics need to check you out."

Bell rested his head next to mine on the grass. "Don't worry. I don't plan to move."

The next two hours were an orderly yet confusing jumble of activity. An ambulance arrived neck-and-neck with the police. We were bundled away in the ambulance to the local hospital to be examined by the E.R. doctor on duty. At the end of the exam, I was told I had a bruised rib, strained right ankle, and bruising just about everywhere that I could be bruised. Bell had a gash on his arm that received seven stitches and an equal number of bruises. The seat belts had saved us from a much worse fate.

We were released with admonitions to take it easy for the next few days and to have our own physicians check us out in a week. After that, we were taken to the police department where we separately gave our statements. Mine consisted mostly of "I don't know." About halfway through my talk with the police officer, another officer came in with a clean shirt, a new pair of jeans and clean sneakers.

"From Mr. Bell," he said with a wry smile. "He asked for a phone call and he called the hotel people. They did some shopping for you."

I thanked him and took the clothing, grateful I wouldn't have to sit too much longer in my damp and smelly clothing. The officer interviewing me took pity on me and handed me over to a female officer who took me to a women's locker room. I washed off with the hand towel she gave me and pulled on the clean blouse and jeans. I mentally applauded Bell on his observational acuity. Everything fit just fine.

I resumed my interview with the officer then I was reunited with my purse, which I had left in the car. While I was wrapping up my talk, Aunt Jane called my mobile phone, alerted by the Small Town Hotline that I was in trouble.

I assured her I was fine but probably not be up to receiving company in a couple of hours. She took charge and told me not to worry about the various cousins coming to town. She would corral them and we would all meet for supper that night. "And if you don't want to come, you stay home," she said before hanging up. "You'll see everybody tomorrow anyway. You get your rest and take care of yourself and Tom."

I breathed a cautious sigh of relief, cautious because it hurt to breathe too deeply. I think I was in shock. Nothing seemed to make sense. Bell said the same thing when I joined him in the lobby of the police station, where he was talking with the two reporters.

"But somebody tried to kill you," Murphy said when I walked up to them. "That's crazy. You should have police protection."

Bell put his arm around me. "The clothes fit. Good."

"Thanks. You think of everything."

He kissed me quickly. "I try. I was just telling the guys, just like I told the police, that police protection isn't necessary in town. You'll stay with me at the hotel tonight and you'll be with your friends and family all day tomorrow."

"Who would do it?" But even as I said it, I knew. Bell's arm tightened around me, telling me that he knew, too.

"Thanks for your help," I said to the two reporters. They were both grass-stained and sweaty looking, but they both also had the excited look of kids who had just been given free access to the candy store. "You got a good story, didn't you?" I said with a smile. "First-hand account about the rescue of Tom Bell and his girlfriend."

Murphy smiled tentatively. "Does this mean you'll do an interview with us?"

"Sure. I'm feeling generous. And bruised," I said pointedly.

"Oh, well, okay. Well maybe after you've had a chance to rest," Billy said. "Later."

"Sounds good. Thanks. I owe you." Bell turned to a police officer who approached us from the offices we'd just left. "All set?"

The man nodded. "In the back, like you suggested."

"I appreciate it. Come on," Bell said to me. "Let's get out of here." He started to follow the officer, taking me with him since his arm was still around me.

"But"—I looked at the front door then back to the two reporters—"where are all the other reporters? A story like this should have them swarming the office."

"The police don't like it when reporters swarm," Bell said. "They kept them outside. I'll talk to you guys later," he said to Murphy and Juko.

"We'll hold you to that." Murphy laughed and the last I saw of him, he and Billy were heading for the front of the building.

We followed the officer. "Where are we going?" I asked.

"I had the car dealer bring me a new car. It's in the lot behind the station. If we hurry, we'll beat the reporters to it. Maybe we can get to the hotel without being bothered."

We did hurry, but it was close. Bell's new SUV was in the parking lot. It was a blue Ford Expedition, an even bigger vehicle than before. I had trouble getting up into it, partly because of bruising and partly because it was so damn tall. The police helped us by having several squad cars exit the lot at the same time we did, holding up traffic from most directions. We managed to get to the hotel and park inside without anyone being the wiser. Or so we hoped.

"I'm surprised no one is staking out the hotel," I said while we climbed wearily up the stairs to his living area.

"The big news is that T.K. Bell was in a car accident then taken to the police station along with the mystery woman in his life. They're all focused on that." Bell went into the kitchen. "I need a drink and a bite to eat. How about you?"

I sank onto his couch. "Sounds good. Double whatever it is you're having."

He busied himself with liquor bottles and the fridge then came to sit next to me, handing me a tall glass full of dark amber liquid then putting a tray of chips and dip on the table. "Here's to us," he said, clinking his glass against mine.

"I'll drink to that." I took a long swallow and expensive bourbon slid down my throat with just a hint of ginger ale.

"Does that mean there is an 'us'?" he asked.

"Hey. I've just been in a major car accident. No fair asking me a question like that." I kept my voice light, but I hope he heard the underlying seriousness.

We were both silent for a moment, munching on chips and busy with our own thoughts. It felt so nice to just sit here. The day had been chaos and this was a haven of quiet and peace. I struggled to keep the memory of the accident out of my mind, but every time I tried, I heard the scream of the metal and felt Bell lunge across the SUV, throwing himself on top of me.

"Why didn't the airbags go off?"

"They're pretty easy to disconnect," Bell said. "All you have to do is know where the fuse box is in the car."

"But when could someone do it? Your car was in my driveway all night."

"And it sat in the garage at the hotel for a month or more since I drove it last." Bell swallowed some bourbon. "I don't have an alarm system at the hotel. I counted on anonymity to keep it private. Maybe I was wrong."

"But how could someone do it?" I insisted.

"Peter was a great mechanic. He was always tinkering with my car. He could do it."

I knew next to nothing about cars, so I took Bell's word for it. "You might have died," I said quietly. "You shouldn't have done that. You shouldn't have unbuckled your seat belt like that. You could have been tossed around so much worse than it was."

He took a swallow of his drink. "I love you, Wendy. I had to do it. There wasn't a choice involved. I had to do it. Why did you stay with me when you might have gotten out?"

I turned my head slowly to look at him. For the third time in as many days, I had that sense of enlightenment, that feeling of *rightness.* "I couldn't leave you alone. It doesn't make any sense, but there it is. I'm not sure what's happening with us, but I think something is."

He smiled slowly, one of his big grins, not the

tight-lipped ones he usually shared. "Does that mean there is an 'us'?"

I leaned over and kissed him. "Quit asking questions."

Chapter 13

I savored my drink, the snacks, and the shower we took, washing away all vestiges of the accident. We were both too beat up to do more than soap each other gently under the spray. The spirit may have been willing but the flesh was very weak. I dressed in one of Bell's clean shirts and we sank onto the bed. I don't know who dropped into sleep first, me or him, but the nap was fabulous.

At five o'clock I nudged him gently. "I have to change my clothes and go meet the cousins," I said, wincing when I stood up.

"You don't like the clothing I selected for you?" Bell asked, hand over his heart in mock pain.

I looked down at the red-and-white checked blouse and blue jeans draped over a chair near the bed. "It's fine. But I'd like to comb my hair, put on some makeup, and get back into funeral mode." My voice was sharper than I meant it to be but I was feeling stressed. The car accident was fading into the background and the reality of Mom's funeral was replacing it. I dressed quickly, using that to avoid looking at him.

"I'm sorry." Bell got up and enfolded me in his arms. "I wasn't thinking, I guess. I'll drive you home and I'll take you to your aunt's place when you're ready."

"I'll be fine. I can drive myself." I shot him a quizzical look. "Unless you're angling for a dinner invitation. You're welcome to join us if you like somewhat overcooked chicken and noodles with a side of limp broccoli."

He laughed. "Sounds delicious, especially since I haven't had a meal since breakfast with you this morning." He released me and pulled on clean jeans and a pale blue shirt. "I'd feel better if I stayed with you, at least until my security team gets here."

"Your security team?" I headed for the door to the living room. "You have your own security people?"

"There's a group I use. They do security for a lot of software companies. They'll get here tonight. Until then, I'm sticking close to you."

"Well, I guess that means you have overcooked chicken in your future." I had to admit, I felt better knowing he was going to be nearby. The accident spooked me. I had never been the victim of a stalker, but I was beginning to feel like one now.

"I got them a couple of rooms here at the hotel so they'll be close by. I want you to sit in on the briefing tonight."

I grabbed my purse from the coffee table and we went to the stairs. "I thought you were sticking to me like white on rice."

"I am."

"Then I'll be at the briefing." I paused on one step to turn and look up at him. "Thanks."

"For what?"

"For taking charge."

"Some women would bitch about that."

"Well, some women aren't me."

He laughed and dashed ahead of me so I ended up falling into his arms at the bottom of the steps. "No kidding."

We drove to my house and surprisingly, there were no reporters camped out on the doorstep. "Where are they?" I asked as we scooted inside.

"I had my PR rep call some newspapers and issue a statement."

I stopped inside the entryway. "You had your PR rep do what? You have a PR rep?"

"It's a marketing firm I hired to do work for me. Whenever I don't want to deal directly with the press, they handle it. And don't forget, Murphy and Jukes got an exclusive story. I'll bet they're being interviewed by their peers right now."

I laughed and walked into the living room, but I came to a stop immediately. "Something's wrong."

Bell stopped behind me. "What?"

"I'm not sure but it feels like things are out of place."

"Close your eyes. Tell me what you should see."

I started to complain but he just squeezed my arm. I sighed and closed my eyes. "Dining room table there." I gestured to the right. "Should be cleared off from this morning's breakfast. The bag of Mom's stuff is on the chair. I think the note she left me is on the table. Straight ahead is the living room. Athos should be on his couch."

"The bag's gone."

My eyes flew open. He was right. The bag full of Mom's safety deposit stuff was gone. "Damn. Did I put it someplace else?"

"No, I think you left it right there." Bell walked

into the dining room.

I went into the living room. Athos wasn't in his accustomed spot. "Where's the cat?" I felt the first touch of panic. Damn it, I couldn't lose Mom's cat. That would be the ultimate capper on a crappy day. "Athos? Where are you? Come on, it's time for dinner," I called. "Come on, kitty. I know you're hungry." I'm sure the cat could hear the desperation in my voice if he was even still in the house. He was an indoor kitty, unaccustomed to the big wide world. Lord knows what would happen if he got out.

I crossed the front entry hallway and went into the downstairs bedroom, the one that Mom and Dad used. Maybe Athos was in Mom's bedroom. I froze in the doorway. "Bell!"

He was by my side in a second. "Son of a bitch," he muttered. "Stay in the living room."

"Like hell I'll stay in the living room." I pushed past him into the mess that was my mother's bedroom. The mattress was pulled off the bed and lay on the floor, the dresser drawers were pulled out and emptied, clothes yanked out of the closet and tossed about. I picked my way through the mess and peered into the bathroom. It was in similar condition.

I glanced over my shoulder. Bell was in the doorway, talking on his cell phone. I reached into Mom's closet and lifted the shoe rack. I tapped the code for the gun safe and opened it. Dad's Smith & Wesson was still inside. I closed the safe and rearranged the shoes, then backed out of the closet.

"Who would do this?" I tiptoed through the debris to Bell, who was talking on his cell phone.

He held up a hand then said, "Okay. I'll meet you

here." He tucked the phone back into his shirt pocket.

"Was that the police?"

"What? Oh, no. I called Jason. He'll meet me here. I'm going to drive you to your aunt's place, Jason will meet me here then we'll pick you up when dinner is over."

"But—"

Bell put a hand on my arm and propelled me out of the room. "Let's go see if your room is like this."

"What? Oh, crapola." I dashed upstairs and made a right turn into my bedroom. It had been searched, too, but less roughly than Mom's room. My suitcase, resting on the trunk at the foot of the bed, was emptied and the drawers on the dresser were pulled out, but most of them were empty anyway. The clothes in the closet were obviously moved around and my small desk in the dormer window nook was in disarray.

"There wasn't as much to search through here since you don't live here anymore," Bell said from behind me. "I'll check the boys' room." He went across the hall and pushed open the other bedroom door. Athos shot out and raced down the stairs in a blur of black and white.

"Well, that explains that," I said, relieved. "I'm glad he didn't get out. I had visions of me wandering through the neighborhood with a can of tuna in one hand."

"He probably ran in here to hide. Looks like this room was searched, too."

I peeked over his shoulder. My brothers' room looked like mine—disturbed but not trashed. "It's been empty for so long. Mom used it for storage, mostly. I suppose that's why it's hardly touched. This doesn't make any sense, Bell. This house has been mostly empty for the last few months because Mom's been in the hospital. I stayed here when I was visiting her, but I was at the hospital most of the time. I don't understand any of this."

"We'll figure it out." Bell put a hand on my back and gently pushed me to my room. "Change your clothes, clean your face, do whatever it was you need to do." He tilted his head to regard me. "You look perfect to me, but I might be prejudiced." Before I could reply, he followed Athos down the stairs. "I'll feed the cat," he called back.

I was too tired to reply. I went into the bathroom at the end of the hallway and regarded myself in the mirror. Thank heavens my bruising was limited to my body, although I looked exhausted, with dark circles under my eyes. And thank heavens I didn't have to do anything to make my hair look relatively decent. I damped down a few recalcitrant strands, washed my face then dabbed on makeup.

I stripped off the clothing Bell had bought me, dropping it on the double bed before consulting my closet. I pulled out a lightweight blue-and-dark-blue striped sweater and dark navy jeans and grabbed a pair of flats from the jumble in the bottom of the closet.

I came downstairs in ten minutes, just as Athos was finishing a dinner of canned tuna on one of Mom's saucers in the kitchen. "I normally don't give him tuna," I said to Bell, who was peering into the fridge. "And he has his own dishes."

"He's had a tough day. He deserves a treat. I think I'll reheat some pizza when I get back here. Some of those casseroles look good, too. You don't mind if I heat one up, do you? Jason and his guys will probably be hungry." Bell straightened and closed the door. Athos took this as a sign that no more food was forthcoming and he sauntered off to sit in the dining room and bathe.

"I don't mind if you eat every casserole in there. The church ladies brought enough to feed an army. How many guys is he bringing?"

"Two. Jason is worth three guys by himself."

"Are we going to tell the police we had a break-in?" I asked.

"I like that," Bell said with a smile. "I like that 'we' you're talking about."

"Quit diverting me. Shouldn't this be reported?" I gestured toward the bedroom, unseen behind the wall behind me.

Bell put a hand on my arm. "Yes, it should be, but I want Jason to look at it before I call in the police. He'll be here in a few minutes, so let's get you to your aunt's place. I want to swing by the hotel and get the notebooks then meet Jason here."

We went outside to Bell's new SUV. "That sedan is gone," I said when I tried to climb into the passenger side. "I need a ladder to get into this car," I grumbled.

"Don't complain. If I need to, I can use it as a battering ram."

We drove the few blocks to the assisted living facility, located not far from the hospital and the hotel. "I'll call you when we're wrapping up." I leaned over the console to kiss him.

"Don't wait for me out here alone." He looked at the long driveway in front of the building. "If you need to wait, make sure to have a cousin or two with you."

"Will do." I paused before sliding out of the SUV. "Thanks, Bell."

He winked. "It's what I do, Wendy. I manage things. Go on ahead and spend time with your family. Everything else can wait."

He was right, of course. It was time to focus on the real reason I was here in town. I was here for Mom. I went into the apartment building to be surrounded by family for the next three hours. I was initially swamped with questions about the car accident, but I managed to downplay it all except to Aunt Jane, who watched me with a sharp eye while I told what had happened. I didn't dare mention the ransacking of Mom's house because that would have caused even more fuss.

Thankfully, talk soon turned to Mom's death, the funeral, and other family members no longer with us. It was a bittersweet reunion because I hadn't seen many of these cousins since the last death in the family, a cousin who died three years previously. We spent the time looking at photographs, talking, and exchanging stories from our childhoods.

Aunt Jane drew me aside when people were starting to leave. "There's more to this than you're telling, isn't there?"

I knew there was no way to evade the truth with her. "It was bad, Aunt Jane. Bell and I were pushed into a ditch filled with water. If two reporters hadn't followed us, I'm not sure what would have happened."

She wrapped her bony fingers around my wrist and held on with surprising strength. "Your mother and your father did everything they could to protect you. I hate to think that all their efforts were in vain all these years later."

I put my hand over hers and squeezed it. "Bell won't let anything happen to me."

She smiled so smugly that I laughed. She laughed, too. "I told you, Wendy Davis. I told you that man would come back into your life. I'm glad you have the good sense to grab him and hold on."

"I'm not sure how long I'll hold him, but it's good to have him here."

She looked at me quizzically. "What's that mean?"

"It just means that I'm not going to plan on a future with someone when I'm in the middle of all this." I raised my hands, taking in my cousins, the scrapbooks, and the memories. I kissed her on one smooth cheek. She smelled of powder and lavender, scents that reminded me of my mother. I put my arms around her and we stood in wordless sympathy.

"Well, don't discount how you feel. It's real, I know it is. You get some rest tonight," she said. "Tomorrow will be a hard day. Don't worry about me. One of the kids will get me to the funeral home for the service. You take care of yourself and take care of Tom."

"I think we're supposed to be there at ten-thirty. The service starts at eleven." I wondered if I had forgotten anything that I was supposed to do. I hadn't even looked at my cell phone lately. I almost pulled it out there to check for messages, but I decided it could wait a few minutes.

Jane patted my arm. "You go, now. Get some sleep. I'll see you at the funeral home tomorrow." She turned to a cousin who was departing and I left, darting into the main lobby where I called Bell.

"We're on our way," he said when I told him the

dinner was wrapping up.

"Some of the cousins are walking to the hotel. Why don't I just go with them and we'll meet there?"

"Do you want to stay there tonight or here at your mom's house?" he asked.

"Did you call the police? Can I stay there or is it a crime scene?" I countered.

"The police have come and gone. I'll fill you in when I see you. Let's meet at the hotel. Just make damn sure you don't walk alone."

"No problem. I have a herd of cousins right here. I'll see you there in a few minutes. I'll wait for you in the lobby." I tucked my phone back into my purse and fell into step with four of my cousins.

It was a glorious night, breezy with a hint of coolness that brought with it the redolent smells of springtime. An almost-full moon was rising, barely seen through the leafed-out trees lining the sidewalks. This was the 'old' part of town and there were still stately Victorian houses with equally stately trees shading them, giving our stroll the feeling of a walk back in time.

Being with my cousins only reinforced that sense of timelessness. How many times did we all get together as children and run around town together? Take our bikes and ride to the swimming pool? Go to the Teen Center and hang out, listening to records? We had ties together that had been stretched by time but not broken. It was reassuring to know I'd have them with me tomorrow, when I had to say good-bye to Mom.

In so many ways my past was fast overtaking me here. Bell had showed up again in my life. Peter might be out there somewhere. I had become reacquainted with the Lost Boys. My cousins were all here, my secondary family, people who had been through so many deaths with me in the past. I thought I was alone, but I wasn't. Even though we were separated by distance, I would always have friends and family.

Bell was a friend who had ties as strong as family ones. I still couldn't quite reconcile my memories of Bell from high school with this take-charge, wealthy man who seemed to be in control no matter what the situation. When our car went over the edge, he thought about me. I was so stunned I couldn't move, but Bell had the presence of mind to get out of his seat belt and protect me. When we were in the ditch and the water was creeping in, he was calm and reasoned, figuring out a solution even as the dirty muck edged higher and higher.

But he had always been like that. The realization settled over me while we neared the hotel, coming up on our right. Bell was one of those people who dreamed impossible dreams and he made them happen. He worked at it and he reasoned it out and he figured out a way to make things work. That probably explained why he was a millionaire and I was plodding along making eighty-thousand a year. He took chances and I didn't.

Another realization followed quickly. I did love Bell, but I couldn't envision a future with him. I just couldn't see this relationship as a permanent thing. I wasn't sure I loved him *that* way. Was I just trying to recreate my past and those astonishing feelings of first love? Or was this real?

"Want to come up for a drink?" my cousin Margaret asked, interrupting my increasingly gloomy thoughts. "We have some wine chilling in the bathroom sink."

"I'm supposed to meet Bell in the lobby. We need go over the accident for his insurance report." It was a lame excuse but the best one I could manufacture to get away from the family gracefully.

"We're in room 150 if you want to come down." We went into the lobby and the cousins headed for the main hallway, calling good-byes back to me.

I sat down in one of the faux leather chairs to the side of the entryway and stared at the TV set, tuned to a news channel. My mind churned, random thoughts popping up. I had to check at home and make sure my funeral clothes weren't all wrinkled from whoever had robbed the place. I may need to do some ironing tonight or tomorrow. I should make a list of what I remembered to be in the safety deposit box sack. I wanted to try to find Mom's correspondence with Bell. Lightly said something about Christmas cards, too, something that made me think I wanted to look at any cards Mom might have around.

Did someone really rob the house? I needed to find out more from Bell about that. Bell. I had to figure out what was going on with him. This *thing* between us couldn't last. It was all a product of stress, worry, and nostalgia. I didn't believe him when he said he loved me. He was feeling the strain of losing Mom, too. He was just facing middle-age and instead of indulging with a young blonde, he fixated on me.

I had totally forgotten about his secret visits to Mom. Why didn't she tell me he was still coming around, years after he had left Kensington? Why didn't she tell me about the drives they took out to the lake? What else didn't she share with me?

That was a disquieting thought. I shoved it aside and considered the notebooks. Did Bell find anything in those old scribblings of Dad's? I glanced at my phone to check the time and that reminded me that I hadn't checked for any messages.

I tapped the phone icon and sure enough, there was a little "1" superimposed on it. I tapped the voicemail icon and put the phone to my ear just as a man came into the lobby and headed straight for me. He was the biggest person I'd ever seen, probably the same size as the football players I saw on TV, with a shaved head, hard-chiseled features, and dressed all in black: jeans, polo shirt, and boots.

"Wendy Davis?" he said, coming to a stop in front of me. "Tom Bell sent me. I'm going to escort you to his quarters."

I stood, phone still pressed to my ear. "Sorry but I don't think it would be smart of me to go with you unless you have some kind of identification." I turned my attention back to my phone and the voice talking.

"Hi, Wendy Darling. I'm looking forward to seeing you."

I recognized that taunting, mocking voice, so soft but also so charged with energy, with smugness.

"Don't tell Tom about this call. If you do, you'll never find out what really happened to your mother. It might be more complicated than you think. How do you think your parents paid for your father's cancer specialist all those years ago? Think about that. And how do you think Bell got the money to start that first company of his? He didn't earn it taking odd jobs here and there. Consider that. I'll talk to you soon. You know where to find me. Bye."

I lowered the phone, Peter's voice echoing in my head.

Chapter 14

"I'm glad you're being cautious," the big man said. He reached into the back pocket of his jeans and pulled out a slender leather ID case, handing it to me.

I took it automatically, my mind trying to digest what I just heard. It was Peter on the phone. He really was alive. I recognized his voice. He had a faint trace of a Southern accent, inherited from his father and his voice was always soft, always suggestive, always with a slight leering quality.

I looked down at the ID. *Jason Simmonds.* The picture matched the giant standing in front of me. "Bell said that having you was like having three guys. I guess he was right. Did you get enough to eat at the house, Mr. Simmonds?"

"Call me Jason, please." He smiled, his granite-like facade cracking. "There's nothing like Church Lady casserole. Yes, we ate well, thank you. Are you ready to go?"

I tucked my phone into my purse. "Sure. It's only a few steps, you know." I started for the front door but he put a hand under my arm and steered me toward the check-in desk. "Where are we going?"

"Special entrance." He nodded to the front desk clerk, a girl who looked high school age. She smiled tentatively in return, looking nervously from me to the big man.

"We're with Tom Bell," I said.

"Oh, well, that's okay then," she said in a rush of relief. The girl moved to the far end of the counter, watching covertly when Simmonds opened one of two doors behind the desk with a key from a bunch hanging on his belt. He ushered me through, turning on a light from a switch on the wall on the right.

I walked forward two steps then stopped. Stairs led downward. "Where does this go?" I waited for him to close and lock the door behind us.

"Tom decided it might be useful to have an additional exit, so when they built the hotel, we had this put in."

"Put what in?" I followed him down the concrete steps. We came to a long, narrow hallway, painted white and brightly lit. There was no hint of dampness or mustiness. The air was as fresh as the air-conditioned lobby above us.

Jason walked down the hallway, speaking over his shoulder while he went. "Tom thought it might come in handy to have another way in and out. He's made a few enemies in his day and it's good to be prepared."

"What?" I hurried to keep pace with him. "What do you mean he's made enemies?"

"You know. Business enemies. Some of them would love to keep track of what he's doing and where he's going." He glanced back at me. "And who he's with."

"Why would any of that matter?"

"Software development is a lot like politics. Perception can be as important as reality. Especially when it comes to shareholders."

I considered prodding him for more information

but decided I'd rather think about the phone call than about any hypothetical enemies Bell had made. Jason slowed his pace and we walked in silence the length of the hotel while my mind churned.

What did Peter mean by that innuendo? When Dad got cancer of the jaw, he did see a specialist, but I assumed it was at the behest of his local doctor and it was all paid for by his health insurance. Peter made it sound like something else was the case. I tried to visualize Mom's files, all neatly categorized in a cabinet in her bedroom. There was one there with a "Medical" label. I would need to pull that out and check it.

"Here we are." Jason opened a metal door and gestured me ahead of him. We emerged into the downstairs portion of Bell's apartment, under the stairs in the rec room. When Jason closed the door, I saw no trace of it at all.

"How did you do that?"

Jason went to the stairs. "Like I said. It's useful to have an escape hatch that nobody knows about." He must have seen my exasperated look because he added, "There's a code pad near the door. That opens it from either side. You must not have seen me use it."

I didn't see him because I was too busy thinking about Peter's phone call. "I suppose that makes sense." I followed him up the steps while I tried to figure out how I'd hide the phone call from Bell. I was never any good at keeping secrets from him.

"How was dinner?" Bell was on the sofa in the living room, my father's notebooks on the coffee table in front of him and a wine glass nearby.

"It was fine. I was glad to get caught up with

people. Probably a good thing you didn't go. You would have been bored silly. What are you doing?" I plopped down next to him.

"I'm going through the stuff your father left."

Jason pulled over one of the arm chairs and sat down. "Jake is on duty downstairs and Bob is at the house."

Bell nodded. "Good. Thanks."

"Who's on duty where?" I looked from him to Jason.

"We had one man watching the apartment where you were having dinner and the other is on duty at your house. Now that you're here, Jake is downstairs, at the garage entrance."

"Good heavens." I sat back. "You act like we're under siege."

"We are." Bell looked at me over his shoulder then turned back to the notebooks. "I'm taking this seriously. You should, too."

"I am. I'm just not accustomed to briefing sessions and guards." I sprang to my feet and went to the kitchen. "Unlike you." I poured myself some wine and sat down again, hoping my nervousness about guards masked my nervousness about Peter. "You know, there's one more thing I don't understand about all this."

Bell sat back and regarded me. "Only one?"

I nudged him in the ribs. "How did the reporters know we were there?"

"There where?" He sipped his wine.

"At the park."

"Oh. That. I didn't give these guys enough credit," Bell said ruefully. "They did their research."

"What's that mean?"

"When I mentioned 'Shadow' to them, they asked around and found out that was our nickname for Peter. Then they dug a bit deeper and found out about the party at Lim's farm where Peter supposedly died. They figured we might go out there again, so they talked to the local real estate agent. You know how local people are. She was so excited because I planned to check the house. They bribed some of the farmers out that way to let them know if an SUV like mine or yours came out. They got the call, they followed us to the house, and they followed us out of the park. Thank God they did."

I shook my head. "I have to admit, I'd be pissed off if I wasn't so thankful they were so sneaky." I looked at the dozen or so Inspiration Spirals then at Jason, unnerved to find him watching me. When I met his gaze, he looked away. "Did you find out anything in Dad's notes?"

"I looked at sections dated one month before and one week before and after the accident at the farm." Bell handed me one dark green notebook with small sticky tabs stuck around the edges like porcupine quills. "I didn't see anything that was about Peter."

"She said something like a week and a month less," I said, opening the notebook at the spots designated by the tabs. "It couldn't be less because that would be before the accident. It has to be a week and a month more, which would be after the accident."

"We figured that out." Bell shrugged when I shot him a dirty look. "I've skimmed through these and I don't see anything about Peter."

"Aunt Jane said it was on Dad's bowling night." I flipped through the notebook, skimming past March. I got to April and stopped, my eye caught by a random phrase on the page.

Specialist might be needed. Does it have to come to that? Dad had crossed out a few words then wrote *Hard to leave my dearest Mary. I know what I leave behind for her. That's what is hardest.*

I looked up, tears spilling down my face. Bell covered my hand with his. "He knew even then that he was sick," he murmured.

"He suspected." I wiped my cheeks. "He was so tired that final year I was in high school. They removed one tumor from his larynx and they thought that was it. He had to do radiation therapy and it made him sick. We assumed that was the cause of his weakness and the pain."

Bell's hand tightened on mine. "I remember that. I would come home to visit and he just didn't have any interest in anything. It was like it was all he could do to get up in the morning and go to the office. When he got home, he was exhausted."

I turned the pages, skimming through the May entries. Dad had jotted figures on pages here and there, long sums of five-digits that didn't make much sense.

"I think that's what it cost for his medical care." Bell tapped the page. "He was adding up what it cost with what they had saved for your college and for John's college."

I swallowed heavily. Was Peter right? How did Mom and Dad pay for that specialist? I just assumed the insurance covered it. God, I was so naive. I assumed so much. "They didn't tell me," I whispered. "I had no idea."

"I don't know if anyone did." Bell slid the

notebook off my knees and turned to the last page in the notebook. "Do you know what this is?"

I shook myself out of my speculative trance and looked down at the scribbles on the page. "Sure. Dad kept track of his bowling scores. I think he had some kind of statistical analysis he did on them to see if he improved or something." I picked up my wine glass and swallowed a healthy amount, trying to rinse away the grief still clinging to me.

"Do you know what this is?" He flipped to another page.

I glanced at it. I was familiar with my father's shorthand when it came to programming. Early artificial intelligence work fascinated him. He taught himself Ada then Prolog, two software languages that were often used in A.I. work. His program designs usually combined elements of the two.

"It's a subroutine," I said. "He always prototyped in Ada."

Bell shook his head. "No, it's not Ada, it's…" His voice trailed off and he lifted his head, staring into space.

"It's Ada," I said, pointing to one line of code. "It's—"

"Wait," Jason said softly.

I had forgotten he was there. I shot him a startled look then I followed his gaze where it was fixated on Bell, who now stared at the notebook. I recognized that faraway look in his eyes. I got up and went to the kitchen, Jason joining me.

"I've seen him do this once before," the big man whispered. "It's like he goes in a trance or something."

"He's in the zone." I took the wine bottle to the

couch and filled Bell's glass, then picked up my glass and rejoined Jason in the kitchen. "It might be a while before he remembers we're here."

"You recognize it?"

"Bell and I go back a long way. I've seen him and my father do all-nighters to debug code. I recognize it." I smiled affectionately at Bell, who was jotting notes on a legal pad on the coffee table. The sight reminded me of the old days, when Dad and Bell would trade ideas while they worked on some gadget or another. Mom would make them sandwiches and they would barely notice her or me or anything around them. We would come back an hour or two later and the sandwiches were gone and the two men didn't even realize they'd eaten.

Did Mom and Dad really take money from Peter and Sylvia so long ago? I sipped my wine, letting my thoughts churn. I suppose it was imaginable, but what wasn't imaginable was that she kept it from me all those years. There were lies within lies and secrets hiding secrets, all tied up with what happened so long ago.

"It's a subroutine," Bell said from the living room. "It's an A.I. subroutine that steps through a man going to spend time with friends then walking home at night, alone."

I nodded slowly. "He hid the information in software code."

Bell smiled. "It's all here." He tapped the notebook.

Jason looked from me to Bell. "What's there?"

"Wendy's father was an amateur programmer. He wrote out a piece of software code that mimics how a

186

human being would behave in certain circumstances."

"Like a robot?" Jason asked.

"Something like." I went back into the living room and sat on the floor, using the coffee table as my desk. I picked up the pages Mom had copied for me. "These are pieces of it." I smoothed down the papers, sorting through them.

"I don't get it," Jason said. He knelt next to me, looking over my shoulder.

"An A.I. program is a series of routines that will make a computer program act like a human." Bell spoke absently, his mind obviously occupied by the pages of the notebook in front of him. "People don't realize it, but our actions are composed of thousands of tiny decision points, many of which have outcomes that follow no logical pattern. An A.I. program attempts to mimic that."

I looked at Jason, whose brow was furrowed so deep it was comical. "It's like this," I said. "Take any action you do. For example, I am thirsty. I don't want water. I want to drink wine. I need to first evaluate my glass. Does it have wine in it or not?"

I held up my glass. "If there isn't wine in the glass already, I branch to a subroutine that takes me into the kitchen to find the wine and fill the glass. If there is wine in the glass, I put my fingers on the glass. I verify that I have wine in the glass to drink. Pick up the glass. Sip from the glass. Is my thirst satisfied? Decide whether to take another sip. Put down the glass." I quickly skimmed the pages in front of me, sorting them into months then weeks then specific days. "I think this is right." I slid the papers across the wooden surface to Bell. "All human activity is a series of cause and effect," I said to Jason. "My father wrote down what happened that night in computer code."

"I still don't get it," Jason said.

Bell tapped the notebook. "This is the master program. It calls subroutines. Wendy's father split all the subroutines into small chunks and inserted them into various spots in the notebooks. Her mother knew what her father did and she reassembled them."

"There's a computer program that proves this guy is still alive?" Jason asked, his skepticism warring with his confusion.

"I need my laptop," Bell told me. "It's in the spare bedroom."

I scrambled to my feet and went into the second bedroom, which also served as an office. Bell's small tablet/laptop sat on the desk next to a stack of folders and books. I grabbed it and turned to leave when light on metal caught my eye.

A gun sat behind the pile of books and papers. It was small and black, probably a 9mm. It was like the one in Dad's gun safe back at the house. Bell had been a security guard at a psychiatric hospital. I suppose that was when he learned to use a gun. He didn't do any shooting when we were dating, at least none that I was aware of. It was perfectly legal in Iowa. The sight of it only reinforced what I knew—there were parts of Bell's life and past that I had no clue about. In many ways, he was a stranger.

I returned to the living room and handed Bell the computer. He pulled a lapboard from behind the couch, opened the laptop, and began to type. I watched him for a second then said, "I still can't believe Peter would do this. He wouldn't try to run us off the road. Why? What does he have to gain from it? Insurance fraud doesn't carry that much of a jail sentence, does it? He could beat that charge, couldn't he?"

"He may have murdered your mother," Bell said quietly. He regarded me for one long minute then returned his attention to his keyboard.

I squeezed my eyes shut, blocking out the image those words invoked. When I opened them, I met Jason's sympathetic gaze. "There's no proof." I was pleased my voice was calm and didn't reflect my inner turmoil. "No one tested her to see if some foreign substance caused her problems." I threw my hands up in the air and went to the kitchen to my glass of wine.

"You don't want to believe that someone you know could murder someone, do you?" Jason said. "Trust me. I've known people to murder other people for a lot less than half-a-million dollars."

"But—" I took a swallow of wine, trying to push my tumbling thoughts into some kind of order. What had Peter meant about 'it's complicated'? What did he mean about my father's cancer specialist?

I looked at Bell and saw him looking expectantly at me. I pushed aside Peter's taunting conversation for later thought. "I grew up with Peter. He was in and out of our house a million times. He knew my parents. He couldn't—" I looked at Bell. "He couldn't kill my mother."

"Who would have believed that I'd grow up in Kensington, Iowa, and go on to become as rich and as famous as I am? Weirder things have happened, Wendy. You have to admit it's at least possible."

"Possible isn't proof. No one has proof. Without that, there's no case. Why would they do it? It makes no sense."

"Let me finish this." Bell shuffled through the pages I gave him, glancing at them then typing. "This might be the proof we need."

"But—"

Jason put a hand on my arm and drew me to his side. "This is personal with him," he said in a low voice. "Let him do it whether it helps or not. Maybe it'll make him feel better."

"If it's personal with anyone it should be me," I whispered in return.

"It's because of you it's personal." Jason nodded when I looked at him incredulously. "Tom cares a lot about you and your family. A lot."

I drained my wine glass and set it in the sink. "Nobody should fight battles for me." I walked into the living room and leaned over Bell. "I'm beat. This day started with a car accident and it's catching up to me."

He kissed me quickly. "I'll be in later. I want to work on this while the ideas are fresh."

I touched his face gently. "I know. I remember." I smiled at Jason. "Tell your guy at my house to feed the cat and don't drink all the beer."

Jason grinned. "Will do. Good night."

I washed away the residue of the day in a warm shower, swallowed three pain/sleep pills then I fell into bed, tossing and turning until I found a position that didn't hurt my bruises too much. I don't know how long I slept but I heard Bell slip into bed beside me.

"Did you get it figured out?" I murmured.

"I think so." He kissed my cheek. "Jason was right. This is personal and it's my fight because of you."

I considered arguing with him but sleep was a

breath away. "We'll talk about it later."

"I mean it, Wendy."

"I'll sleep on it, Bell." I closed my eyes and turned over.

"I won't let you get away again," he said softly. "I mean it."

It almost sounded like a threat. I filed that away for later worry. Right now, all I wanted was temporary unconsciousness.

I woke early in the morning, just as it was getting light. I lay in the unfamiliar bed, trying to catch my bearings. Then I heard Bell next to me, his breathing heavy.

Bell. Good Lord, what was I going to do about him? I propped myself up on my elbows and peered at the window. Sunlight was creeping in. It would be a good day for Mom. That was what was important. I slid the covers off and sat up.

"Wendy?"

I looked over my shoulder. Bell lay on his side, watching me. "We need to talk sometime. About our future."

"We don't have a future, Bell." I saw the protest in his eyes and I hurried on. "I love you. But that doesn't mean we have a future together."

"You're not talking sense. You're upset. It's everything that's happened. We can talk about it later."

"That's exactly why it makes sense." I slid away from his touch and stood, picking up the shirt I was using as a robe. "We got back together at a time of extreme stress. It's a lot of nostalgia mixed in with fear that makes us want to be together."

"That's bullshit. I love you, Wendy."

191

"If you loved me, why didn't you get in touch with me before this?"

He didn't answer immediately then finally said, "I had to prove myself. I wanted to be a success."

I blinked widely in surprise. "Bell, you're the very definition of success."

"Yeah," he said wryly. "It was your mom who finally made me realize that. And she made me realize that I needed to take a chance and approach you again."

"But you never did."

"I was going to. Then she died and…It wasn't until I saw you again that I realized how much I do love you."

I headed for the bathroom. "It wasn't until you saw me again that you realized how much you once loved me. You're just trying to recreate that feeling, Bell. It isn't real."

"Is that how it is for you?" he asked.

He looked so hurt, so disconsolate, that I almost dropped my clothes and went back to the bed. "I don't know what it is with me," I said quietly. "I do know that my mother's funeral is today and I want to focus on that. You and I will just have to wait, Bell. Today is Mom's day. I need to go home and get ready."

"I'll go with you."

"No, I'd like some time alone."

"I want to keep a guard with you."

I shook my head. "I really want some time alone."

He shook his head just as adamantly. "I want a guard with you. You know and I know that wasn't an accident yesterday."

I relented. I knew there would be no convincing him. "OK. Whatever." I headed for the bathroom.

"We'll talk about this later," he called after me.

"I'm sure we will," I muttered.

Half an hour later I was in the car with a man with a shaved head and muscles on top of muscles, who looked like an ex-prize fighter. He was introduced to me as Bob, the guard who had stayed at the house the night previously. We drove to the house in a maroon Cadillac sedan that Bell had rented 'because it looks better than the truck for a funeral.' I was relieved I wouldn't have to climb in and out of his monster truck.

When Bob and I neared the house, I saw the car sitting across the street in the same position it had been in the day before. "I need to talk to the person in the car," I said when Bob pulled into the driveway.

"I'll come with you." He shut off the engine.

I hopped out of the car and was halfway across the street before he got out. I held up a hand when he started to follow. "Stay there. I just need a minute." I didn't give him a chance to protest but I walked over to the sedan and tapped on the glass.

The window rolled down.

"Hello, Peter," I said.

Chapter 15

The shape of his face was different, but he still had that distinctive sandy-red hair, straight and fine, cut shorter now and framing his face. He also had the same crafty, pale blue eyes that I remembered from long ago. When we were younger his face was a perfect oval, with high cheekbones that accented his long, patrician nose. Now his face was rounder, his eyes slightly slanted down at the corners, giving him a sad, almost pensive look. But his mouth was the same. Peter had a very deep indentation above his lips as well as a small chin. It used to make his face appear somewhat unbalanced and bottom-heavy, but now his thinning hair gave him more forehead, balancing out the look.

All of this flashed through my brain in the time it took to recognize him. He smiled, that distinctive one-sided almost-sneer of his. "Hello, Wendy. Good to see you."

"It's not good to see you, Peter. What do you want?"

"I want the proof. I want to make sure it's destroyed."

"I don't have any proof," I countered.

"You must have it. I know how your father was. He would document it. That means you must have it, now that your mother's dead." His smile hardened into a sneer. "She felt guilty, although I don't know why. I

194

suppose it was because she took the money from us. And because of Tom Bell, of course."

"What?" I leaned on the car, as much to get closer to him as to block the sunlight glaring into my eyes. "What about Bell?"

"Your mother took money from us then Tom tried to pay it back. He and your mother became accessories to murder. Then Tom got the bright idea to try to blackmail me. If I go to jail, he goes to jail. Even if you don't care about Tom, do you care about your mother? Of course, it doesn't matter to her now, but do you care about her reputation?"

"I don't believe you," I said.

"Your father saw me that night. Your parents needed money. Your father's job paid him a pittance and they had kids to put through college. Then your father got sick and he had more bills to pay. But why am I telling you this? I'm sure you knew." His pale eyes reminded me of the blue glass marbles my brothers used to play with. They looked equally hard and cold.

"You said 'us'. Is your mother here, too?" I was stalling, struggling to make sense of what he was saying.

"She wanted to come but we decided that I should handle it. To be honest, her joy at attending your mother's funeral might have been a giveaway. My mother hated your mother. She always said your mother acted so perfect it was sickening. The perfect Susie Homemaker." Peter looked past me, where I'm sure Bob the guard was watching us. "Meet me later."

"I can't. We have the memorial service then I have to be with family this afternoon."

"Is the burial private or public?"

"She was cremated. It's an inurnment. It's private. Just me and Aunt Jane."

"What time?

"Five o'clock."

"Perfect," he said. "Bring it to the cemetery. I'll meet you there." He rolled up the window just as Bob joined me.

"Everything okay?" he asked.

I stepped away from the car. "Yes. Just an old family friend who couldn't come to the funeral." I walked to the house, my legs so stiff and wooden I'm surprised I could climb the stairs to the back door.

Athos wandered into the hall. At first I thought he was meeting me, but he deftly sidestepped my ankles and went to Bob. "We're friends. We sort of bonded last night." Bob bent to touch Athos' head and despite my worries, I smiled at the sight of the big, burly man and his gentle pat on the small cat's head.

"I'm going upstairs to change." I headed for the living room and the stairs. "Make yourself some coffee and toast or whatever."

"There's a good breakfast casserole in there." He cast a longing look at the fridge.

I waved a hand. "Help yourself. Good casserole should never go to waste."

He nodded enthusiastically and went into the kitchen, Athos at his heels. I paused at the doorway to Mom's bedroom. It wasn't the chaotic mess it had been yesterday. Someone had tried to make it look at least somewhat normal. The mattress was back on the bed, the drawers were closed, and the closet looked disorganized but tidy.

There was something I was going to look for, but I couldn't remember what. Something in Mom's files or her papers. I shook my head. I couldn't keep anything straight any more. Words, days, events were all getting jumbled in my brain. I felt as though I'd gone from crisis to crisis since Tuesday, when Bell met me at the cemetery. I didn't have any time to sit and evaluate everything going on.

I started to leave then stopped. Common sense warred with worry. Worry won. I went to the gun safe, tapped in the code and pulled out Dad's gun. The magazine was nestled in the foam next to the handgun. I checked the weapon, which looked as clean and ready as it did back when Dad and I would go out to the woods and practice. He had insisted that all of us, Mom included, know how to handle a gun safely.

Some lessons are never forgotten. I took the gun and the magazine and started to leave the room. That's when I remembered I wanted to look through Mom's files. I went to the desk in the corner and opened the bottom drawer. Neatly labeled manila folders were lined up in a staggered, orderly fashion. I pulled out the one marked 'Correspondence' and one marked 'Medical' then closed the drawer.

I turned to go but glimpsed her address book on the desk top. I took it, too and went upstairs and into my bedroom. I put the files and address book on the bed and picked up my funeral purse, lying on the trunk at the foot of the bed. It was divided, a black bag with an open center section and two zippered side sections. I loaded the gun, made sure the safety was on then tucked it into the center section, where it was easily hidden under a handkerchief. I had no idea if I'd need it or not, but it felt right to have it with me.

Next I checked my outfit for the day. Whoever had vandalized the house left most of my things alone. I sighed with relief when I verified the black slacks and black-and-white polka dot sweater were unwrinkled and clean.

Well, at least one worry was put to rest. I showered and dabbed on makeup, disjointed phrases flitting through my mind. Bell had an adoptive daughter in Europe. Peter had perhaps murdered my mother. Bell was ceding all rights to an app to me. I had Money with a capital M. Peter claimed my mother blackmailed him. Bell was predictable when it came to me. Otherwise, he was unpredictable. Totts and the others had fooled us all, keeping Peter's secret for decades.

Thinking about secrets reminded me. I went to the bedroom and opened the file folders. The Medical folder had several bunches of invoices. I skimmed through them quickly, but they were all for Mom's expenses, not Dad's. I stared thoughtfully into space. Where would she keep his papers? Maybe there was another folder I missed.

I turned to the Correspondence folder and found Christmas cards and letters from various people. I sorted through them, recognizing some names. I was bundling them all back into the folder when one caught my eye. It was a stylized Christmas card, edgy and modern looking. I opened it.

Sylvia Barry was engraved inside under a banal inscription.

Mom got a Christmas card from Sylvia. Why? I checked her address book and sure enough, in the B section was a notation for Sylvia Barry and an address in California. Next to the name was last year's date. Mom always noted when she sent someone a Christmas card, so presumably she sent Sylvia a card.

And it was just a month or so later that Mom was sick and lying in the hospital, paralyzed and unable to communicate. Were the two connected?

They had to be. I got dressed, barely noticing what I was doing. What kind of proof did Peter want? I had no proof and as far as I knew, Mom didn't either. What was that crack Peter made about Dad? Did Mom contact Sylvia?

Maybe this was all bullshit and Peter was just trying to fool me into giving him whatever we had. Wait a minute. I didn't have anything. Bell had all the notebooks and papers. Damn. I sat on the bed. I left everything with Bell.

Was Bell a blackmailer? Good God, what was real and what wasn't? I stood up and stared at myself in the mirror. Was I real? I felt so unreal, preparing for my mother's funeral with this turmoil going on around me.

I took a deep breath. Milestones. That's the thing. Focus on one thing at a time. The funeral. That's the next thing. Everything else will work itself out. Get through the funeral first. I left the room and stopped at the top of the stairs, remembered words filtering back to me.

Peter was great at predictive analysis. Peter's girlfriend died in California. Peter. It all came back to him. He had been the unofficial leader of The Lost Boys, the charismatic Pied Piper who led everyone— except Bell.

There was something niggling at my mind, some idea or fragment that wanted attention. I tried to recall it, but as soon as I did, the idea vanished. I walked down the steps, forcing everything else out of my mind except the ordeal ahead. Everybody and everything was secondary. I had a funeral to endure.

Bell, Jason, and Bob were all in the dining room, talking quietly. Jason and Bell wore suits, Bell's dark gray and Jason's black. They looked dignified and so grown-up. For an instant I felt out of place, like I didn't belong. I had intruded on the adults, all talking so softly.

I recognized the feeling. Whenever I came home to visit, I had that dual feeling of being mature and yet young. I could act like an adult to strangers, but to Mom I was still her kid. All that was gone now. Now I'd have to be a grown-up all the time. It was a chilling thought.

"Ready?" Bell asked when he saw me.

I nodded. "You'll sit with us, right?" I asked.

"Of course."

I led the way to the back door, my black leather purse slung tightly across my shoulder and pressed to my side. I paused once and looked back. Bob smiled tentatively at me, but I barely noticed him. This was Mom's home. Everything would be different when I came back.

I walked outside and automatically checked across the street, where the car sat just an hour or so earlier. "Where are the reporters?" I followed Bell to the Cadillac in the driveway.

"I told them that if anyone showed up at the funeral I'd see to it they never work again." Bell looked as grim as he sounded. He held open the front passenger door for me. "I think they believed me."

I slipped into the car and dense silence surrounded me. Bell and Jason spoke briefly outside the car then Bell got into the driver's seat. "Jason will follow in my truck and he'll stay in the back at the service. Bob will stay in place at the house. Jake is in place at the hotel."

"Do you think that's necessary? Surely no one would try anything in public, would they?"

"I'd rather not take any chances." Bell backed down the driveway and we drove in silence for a minute. "Thank you for letting me be part of the family today. Your parents were an important part of my life."

"Thank you for helping me. I'm not sure what I'd have done without you."

"It's probably because of me that things are happening." He drove slowly, keeping an eye on the rear-view mirror. I spied Jason following in Bell's new SUV. Like Bell, he seemed to be looking around, as though expecting someone to jump out at any moment.

"Are you sure? Maybe I'm the bad luck magnet, not you." I glanced at the dashboard clock. It was almost ten-thirty. I tried to swallow but my throat was suddenly dry. I closed my eyes and scenes from my past flowed by. Memories of picnics with the family, my father and mother laughing together, evenings spent roughhousing on the floor in the living room.

You were always so predictable. Bell said that, but Mom said it once, too. *I can always count on Wendy Darling,* she used to say. *You were always so predictable.* That's why the app was a success. You were so predictable until people made you unpredictable.

Peter was a predictive genius. He analyzed people and predicted how they would act. Bell knew that. *You were always so predictable.* This was a game to them. It was personal for them, especially for Bell, if he was a blackmailer.

I drew in a startled breath. How could I think such a thing? Even when I chided myself, I knew it was a possibility. Bell had a tough, sharp side. He'd blackmail Peter in a heartbeat if he felt it was necessary.

"Where should I park?"

Bell's quiet words woke me from my trance. "In the side lot. There's a spot there reserved for family."

He parked the car. I sat for a minute, waiting for him to come around to my side, using the time to gather my emotions. When Bell opened the door for me, I got out, noticing Jason had parked at the far end of the lot, near the exit. He sat in the truck, watching us and the entrance to the funeral home.

The service was in the funeral home's "chapel," a large room with rows of chairs lined up. Aunt Jane was in the small receiving room at the back, seated in one of the armchairs near the fireplace with several cousins nearby. I joined her, Bell following me.

"Aunt Jane, this is Tom Bell. I'm not sure if you remember him or not."

She held out her hand, looking like a queen giving permission for a knave to kiss it. "Of course, I remember you, Tom. I'm glad you're here." She introduced my cousins while I spoke with the funeral director, a calm, respectful man that I remembered from high school. He was my younger brother's age and it was comforting yet odd to have him handling all the arrangements. I again had that confusing feeling of being a child at a grown-up function.

The music I chose for Mom began to play and

people filed into the meeting room in front of us. We were buffered from the crowd by bi-fold doors, but I heard the murmur of voices and shuffling feet while people were seated. Several family friends came in to see Aunt Jane or me, and so began the ritual of hugs, kisses, tears, and greetings, all overlaid with a comforting air of fellowship in the truest sense of the word. All of us had lost loved ones. We all knew how each other felt. Love and support surrounded me on all sides, especially because Bell was near me the entire time, talking quietly to people, sharing memories, and gently steering conversation away from the morbid to happier talk.

A few minutes before the service started, my cousins filed into the chapel. Aunt Jane stood and slipped her arm through mine, clasping me tightly. "I will miss her terribly," she said softly. "I would hate to think that someone cut short her time on this earth." She looked past me to Bell when she said it. "It would comfort me a great deal to know that if someone did cause Mary distress, they would pay for it."

"I'm sure they will, ma'am." Bell fell into step behind us, his gaze intersecting mine. "I'm sure they will."

"Don't promise something you can't deliver," I whispered over my shoulder.

"I can deliver." He smiled coldly.

The funeral director opened the bi-fold doors. Jane and I stepped out into the chapel, walking slowly down the aisle between the rows of chairs. The place was packed with every chair taken and many people standing at the back. I expected that. Mom and Dad had been a part of the town all their lives and the town would turn out to say good-bye.

I glimpsed Totts, Dibs, and Lightly all sitting together near the back, not far from Jason, who stood near the door, looking large and somber. I tried to smile but it came out more like a grimace, I think. I moved slowly, letting Jane set the pace, and she paused now and again to nod or acknowledge someone. We finally reached the front of the room and took our seats in the "family" section. Bell followed, sitting next to me on my left.

The minister from Mom's church sat in front near a podium from which he would officiate. It was a compromise to have him there. Mom was adamant that she didn't want a church service, but she liked the minister. When I asked him to lead the ceremonies, he readily agreed even though it wasn't located in his church. I was relieved to have someone running things who knew what to do.

Once we were all settled, the minister stood. "I welcome you all here to celebrate the life of Mary Ansell Davis, who was a wife, mother, and member of our community. Mary was active in all walks of Kensington life, serving on the library board, the PTA, and other volunteer committees." He went on to summarize the many activities that occupied my mother through the years.

A girl soloist from the high school then stood and sang *Bridge Over Trouble Waters,* a song which had me dabbing at tears. I glanced covertly at Jane, but she appeared composed, her face serene. I thought of all the funerals we had attended over the years and gathered a measure of strength from her.

The minister next spoke a few verses from the

Bible, ones which really didn't seem very relevant to me but which apparently struck the right chord with the audience because they listened with rapt attention. After that the minister read Mom's Summary, as she called it. She had written it herself, just a straightforward recitation of her birth, marriage, children, and life. It didn't sum up for me all she had accomplished, but it was what she wanted so I left it alone.

After that the soloist sang *Yesterday*, another song that made me teary. Bell clasped my hand and I leaned my head on his shoulder, letting tears roll down my face. It felt as though my past was being slowly peeled away from me, one teardrop at a time.

The minister then spoke about Mom and Dad, giving little anecdotes about their life in town and their involvement in so many town events and festivals. People must have shared their memories, because we all laughed several times at the stories he told about parade floats gone awry or a car that refused to start so a tractor had to be conscripted to drive the Homecoming Queen around town. He described our Christmas holidays, when all the Lost Boys would gather and we would sing Christmas carols then the kids would go tobogganing down Dead Man's Hill and how Dad would often be called out to haul someone to the doctor.

His words painted the picture of a happy time, a time before mobile phones and email. My parents truly had been the ringleaders to our rag-tag group of kids, always managing to show us how to have fun on such a limited budget. I glanced back at Totts and the others and received answering smiles. They had the same memories I did. Perhaps my past was being peeled away from me, but not completely. I would always have the core of it, the love that my parents shared.

When he finished speaking, the minister stepped back. A woman from Mom's bridge club came forward and gave a short talk about Mom's interaction with them through the years, once again bringing forth smiles and chuckles at some of the things she said. Then the town librarian spoke, telling about Mom's tireless work on the library board of directors.

When she sat down the minister nodded to Bell, who gently let go of my hand then stood, straightening his suit before walking to the podium. Bell nodded politely to the minister then he turned to face the crowd, his hands gripping the sides of the wooden platform. Bell's pale green eyes scanned the faces, a faint smile on his face, then he looked at me, and I saw the love in his gaze before he began to speak.

"George and Mary Davis welcomed me into their home when I was a child. They treated me as though I was their son. I can't tell you how much that meant to me. When I first met the Davis family, I was wild and undisciplined. My mother struggled to raise me correctly, but without my father in the picture, she had all she could do just to make ends meet. When I was accepted into the Davis household, I learned what it was to be part of a family."

Bell paused and looked around the audience, making eye contact with several people. He spoke smoothly and confidently. I wondered if he'd practiced this. If he hadn't, he did a good job because he spoke without notes and without any hesitation.

"They accepted me for what I was—a poor kid from the wrong side of the tracks. They treated me the same way they treated their own kids. I had rules to follow and chores to do. I couldn't just come over to the house and freeload. Everybody worked and that was just the way it was. I wasn't a guest there. I was one of them." He smiled wistfully and I glimpsed several people in the audience nodding.

"They taught me to believe in myself. George showed me that I had skills and talent. I wasn't just a nobody. I had a chance to make my mark in the world if I would only work at it. Mary taught me how to be, well, how to be human, I guess you could say. She showed me that it wasn't weakness to be kind to people. She taught me that it was safe to love someone because even if the love isn't returned, it isn't wasted." Bell's gaze settled on me then moved away. Jane took my hand and squeezed it once, then released it and patted my arm in consolation.

"In later years, I often visited Mary and it was like coming home for me. I've spent a lot of time in big cities and working on big projects, but when I came back to Kensington, I was just Tom Bell, the same kid who ran in and out of her house with the other boys. I was still important, but in a different way. I was important because Mary loved me, not because I was rich or famous." He looked down at the podium for a long moment, obviously struggling to control his voice. "That's the best kind of important to be and they shared that with me. I will be forever grateful to them for that."

He looked around the crowd, his gaze moving slowly from one side to the other then settling on me. "Mary's life is truly a celebration of everything she believed in. We'll miss her but she left us something precious and rare. She gave us unconditional love. It's a gift I'll always cherish."

Bell stepped back from the podium and nodded to the minister, then walked to his seat next to me. I reached for his hand. "Thank you," I whispered. "You said what I couldn't."

He raised my hand and kissed it, then nodded. "I know."

Two simple words. *I know.* Once again, I had that wild epiphany, that feeling of *rightness* which had been warring with my common sense since Bell reappeared in my life. He did know how I felt. He did understand without me telling him.

The minister said a prayer and gave a benediction then it was over. The pianist started to play and as Jane, Bell, and I left, the soloist began singing *Bird on a Wire,* the Leonard Cohen song my mother loved. I smiled through my tears at the lyrics. It was such a fitting end to her leave-taking.

I walked out into a world bright with sunlight, feeling like a new page was turning in my life. My mother would always be a part of me, but now I truly did need to decide for myself what direction my life would take.

I felt Bell's arm around my shoulders and I turned to smile at him. That's when I saw Peter, leaning against a car across the street.

Chapter 16

The sight of him reminded me of my dilemma, which I had successfully forgotten during the memorial service. I needed 'proof' of some kind that Peter would believe. Peter smiled when he saw me and ducked into his car.

I had to come up with something. The thought nagged at me as Bell opened the door for me and I sat in the passenger seat. He slid behind the driver's wheel and started the engine. "Country Club, right? For the luncheon?"

I nodded, hoping he'd take my silence for grief instead of confusion. There wasn't any hearse because Mom was cremated, so the funeral director led the way in his sedan with Aunt Jane and some of the cousins. Bell pulled into line behind them and other cars followed us out of the parking lot.

Peter said he wanted proof or else—or else what? I turned toward my window and closed my eyes, letting the filtered sunlight cause starbursts to go off behind my eyelids. It was a checkmate, wasn't it? Peter wanted proof or else he'd go to the police. But he couldn't go to the police without confessing to insurance fraud.

Did he really think I wouldn't come to that conclusion? I rubbed my forehead, trying to find logic behind what was probably the empty threats of a petty criminal.

"Headache?" Bell asked, glancing my way.

"I just don't know what to believe anymore." I rested my head back on the seat. "Blackmail, murder, lies. What's true and what isn't?"

We drove for a minute in silence then Bell asked, "Who said anything about blackmail?"

My eyes flew open. "I don't know. I guess I just—" I stammered to a halt. "I don't know."

"Has something happened you haven't told me about?" His voice was mild but I thought I heard underlying irritation.

"Has anything happened that you haven't told me about?" I countered. "What did you find in Dad's notes? Was there any concrete proof that Peter is alive? Or was there just the program, the pseudo-code?"

"That's enough, isn't it?"

"For who? It may be enough for you and me, but it won't be enough for the police." I tried to think of some subtle way to ask him about how he got his starting money in business. I gave up when everything I considered sounded too obvious. "We have no proof that anyone did anything to harm Mom and we have no proof that Sylvia and Peter conspired to defraud the insurance company. This has all been a waste of time."

"All of it?" Bell glanced at me before turning into the long drive leading to the Country Club, an unpretentious establishment on the northeast side of town. "Do you mean that you and me are a waste of time?"

"I didn't say that."

"You've been acting like we're not important, acting like what's between us is temporary and unimportant. Is that how you really feel?"

I blew out an exasperated sigh. "Would you give it a break? I can barely think straight much less make emotional decisions that may affect the rest of my life. Give me some time to figure out how I feel."

He parked next to the funeral sedan. "You shouldn't have to figure it out, Wendy. You should just know." Bell stared ahead through the windshield, his mouth set in a tight, angry line. "If you need to think about it, then I guess I have my answer."

He threw open his door before I could reply. I didn't wait for him to come around the car. Instead, I opened my door and went to join Aunt Jane, who stood next to the funeral sedan. She put an arm around my shoulders in a brief hug. "Troubles, dear?" she asked softly, looking from me to Bell, who waited near the entrance to the clubhouse, his head down and shoulders hunched.

"I don't know," I said. "It's not important."

"It's important. It's just not timely, that's all." She tucked her arm through mine and we went into the clubhouse, with Bell and my cousins following us.

The Kensington Country Club was a club located in the country, but it was a far cry from the elegant country clubs in bigger towns. The clubhouse was just a two-story wooden building with locker rooms and a scarred and battered bar downstairs and a large banquet room upstairs. It was often used for funeral lunches because it the only place in town large enough to host more than thirty people.

I got Aunt Jane settled at the main table near the doorway and I went to check on the catering arrangements. The church ladies had everything well in hand, so I rejoined Jane and Bell. He sat next to her and they were talking so earnestly I was certain I was the topic of their conversation, a thought confirmed when they hushed up as soon as I neared.

"Go ahead," I said, taking a seat on Jane's other side. "You know you want to tell me how to run my life, so just go ahead and do it."

"I was just saying that I wondered what your mother would think of all this fuss," Jane said placidly. "She never cared to be the center of attention."

"Hmm. I could have sworn you'd be talking about me."

Jane patted my arm. "There's nothing to discuss, dear. You're very predictable." She turned to talk to someone behind us.

I was glad she couldn't see my face. If one more person told me I was predictable, I'd stand up and scream. I was sick to death of that being thrown in my face like it was a vice. What if I was cautious? What if I was careful? I fumed for a minute or two then forced myself to be polite to the well-wishers who stopped by the table to chat.

Maintaining a polite facade got me through lunch, and with Jane between me and Bell, I didn't have to worry about saying something wrong or hurting his feelings. I felt like a fraud, chatting with mourners while another part of my mind was trying to figure out a way to handle Peter.

Maybe that was a mistake. Maybe I just needed to meet with him and call his bluff. The more I thought about it, the better that idea sounded. Peter really had no threat to hold over me. If I didn't cooperate, he wasn't going to go to the police. Doing so would reveal his fraud.

In fact, I thought, maybe I should call the police. They could come to the cemetery and arrest him. I considered that idea in between bites of casserole and Jell-O salad. Then I remembered. Peter said Bell was blackmailing him. What if that came out? Of course, what if Peter was lying? My head hurt. I couldn't keep fact, innuendo, and accusations straight any more.

"Are you okay?"

I snapped out of my reverie. Lightly had taken an empty seat beside me and was looking at me, worry apparent on his handsome face.

"I'm just tired." I rubbed my forehead. "I have a headache and this day feels like it's lasting forever." I wasn't sure if he knew about our accident, so I didn't mention the bruising and overall achiness I was also feeling.

"I know. It can be wearing. You're almost done, though. Most of the people are leaving."

I looked around the room. He was right. The crowd was thinning out. A few older ladies were grouped around Aunt Jane, who had moved to another table. When she saw me, she waved me to her. "I'm being paged," I said. "Thanks for coming. I appreciate it."

Lightly squeezed my hand. "Your parents always made us feel welcome. It's the least I could do, to come here and share some memories." He smiled and moved off.

I went to Aunt Jane and helped her to her feet. "I'm going back to lie down," she said. "I talked to Reverend Roberts. He said he'd drive me to the cemetery. You'll meet me there at five o'clock?"

"Are you sure?" I looked at Bell, who was talking to the Lost Boys near the door. "We can drive you out.

You don't need to go with the minister."

She gave me a brisk hug. "I think you and Tom could use some time alone. Besides, I want to come back right after the service and visit with some of the family. I think you'll probably want to be there longer than me. Why don't you and Tom come over to my apartment when you're ready to relax tonight?"

"Thank you. I'd like that." I kissed her cheek and watched her leave with one of my cousins providing her with a strong arm for support. Jane may have looked and acted younger than her age, but she was almost eighty and this day had taken a toll on her.

Bell rejoined me. "Are you ready to go?"

I nodded. "I'm beat. I think I'd like to lie down, too."

"I'll drop you at the house. I have some things to do. Bob is still there, but he'll stay out of your way. I'll come back and get you a little before five so we can go to the cemetery."

"You don't have to go with me," I said. "I can ride out with Aunt Jane."

"I'd like to go, unless you'd rather I didn't." He sounded formal, distant.

"No, that's fine." I was too tired to argue about it. I had no idea how I would get rid of Bell and Aunt Jane so I could talk to Peter. I'd just have to figure out something. I made my thanks to the ladies from the church who arranged the lunch, then chatted with the funeral director and some guests who remained. It was two-thirty by the time Bell and I left.

"Are you sure it's okay if I come with you to the cemetery?" he asked while we drove to the house.

"I'm not trying to exclude you, if that's what

you're asking. I'm just not sure that you'd want to be there. It will be a very short service."

We drove past a small park and I glimpsed a couple of adults watching children play on swing sets. School was still in session so they must have been preschoolers. They all looked so carefree and happy. I felt as though I'd been carrying a weight for days on end. Peter, Bell, my mother's death, the money from the app—my life was turned upside down in four days and I wasn't sure what shape it would be in when it finally righted itself.

"I get the feeling there's something going on you're not telling me about." Bell's voice was soft and politely accusatory, as though he was probing for more information.

"If I'm not telling you about it, then there's probably a reason," I shot back. "You treat me like I'm an idiot child sometimes, Bell. Can't I have a life?"

His mouth thinned into an imperceptible line. "That's offensive."

"What is?"

"That crack about an idiot child."

I stared at him, puzzled. Then I remembered the child he adopted. "I'm sorry. I forgot about your—your past."

"She's my daughter. I adopted her. Why is that so hard for you to remember?"

"I've had a bit of stress in the last few days. Why is it so hard for you to remember that?" His accusation stung, partly because he was right. I should have remembered about his daughter, but I had completely forgotten. It was obviously important to him and it should have been important to me.

215

We drove in silence to the house. Bell pulled in behind my car, sitting in the drive. "I'll pick you up at four-forty-five," he said.

I nodded and opened the door.

"Wendy, I'm sorry. I know you're under a lot of stress. I am, too. I'm just not used to sharing with someone. I guess I'm out of practice." He looked and sounded honestly contrite.

I recognized a gesture of peace when I saw it. "I'm sorry, too. I don't mean to be ungrateful, but it's been a long time since I had to report in to someone."

"You don't have to report to me. I was just hoping you'd share with me, that's all."

"I have, Bell. As much as I can right now."

He smiled tentatively. "I'll see you later."

"Okay." I slipped out of the car before he could interrogate me further. I was never any good at keeping secrets from him and I had no reason to think that had changed.

Bob opened the door for me when I neared it. "All quiet here," he said when I passed by him into the dining room.

"Good. I'm going to lie down for a while. Don't interrupt me unless the house catches fire, okay?"

"Will do."

I felt his eyes on me while I crossed through the living room and climbed the stairs. I went into my room and dropped onto the bed, my purse sliding to the floor next to me. I stared at the ceiling for a minute then closed my eyes, trying to will away the insistent headache pounding through my brain. All I wanted was oblivion. Just a short hour or so of relaxation and forgetfulness. I wanted to put all anxiety, all worry behind me.

As soon as I thought that, I realized how futile a hope it was. I put my arm over my eyes and for the first time I wept completely, big hot tears that burned while they rolled down my face. I was alone. Mom had always been there, just a phone call away, a constant presence in my life. She was the person I could always visit, that voice at the end of the phone. Now there was nothing.

True, I had Bell. But it wasn't the same. This was a loss of my past, my childhood, and my adolescence. If I wasn't careful, this would push me toward Bell even more. I had to be careful. I had to be objective. The things I felt now were a residual of my loss of my mother. I just had to let him know this wasn't a permanent thing.

And Peter—what to do about Peter?

"The hell with it and the hell with him," I muttered. I was tired of thinking about it. I'd worry about it later.

****

Now it was later. I woke after a fitful ninety-minute nap and washed my face and changed clothes into black jeans and flats, more appropriate for the cemetery. I replaced my handkerchief in my bag and verified the gun was still there then I slung the purse over my shoulder and went to the window.

The previous blue skies and puffy white clouds were replaced by blue-gray skies with low-hanging bruised-looking clouds. I considered grabbing an umbrella, then decided I was at the end of a long, horrible day. What did it matter if I got wet?

I went downstairs. Bob sat in the living room near Athos on the couch. Both looked up when I entered.

"Did you get a nap?" Bob asked.

I nodded. "I feel better now. This must be pretty boring for you, just sitting around waiting for something to happen."

"That's a lot of what security is. Hours of boredom interrupted by moments of terror. You get used to it." He held up a computer tablet, which looked as small as a smartphone in his big hand. "I always have a bunch of books loaded and ready to go, so I'm never really bored."

"I'm going to make some coffee. Want some?"

"I already have a pot going." He got to his feet and followed me, pausing in the dining room when I went into the kitchen. I poured myself a mug of coffee and joined him at a seat at the table.

"How long have you guys worked for Bell?" I asked between sips.

"About ten years now. We're not full-time for him. We're just on call for when he needs us. You know, for special events or when there's a threat."

"A threat?"

"He's gotten a few threats over the years. Usually some crackpot who has a grudge or something. It doesn't happen too much now that those crazy people in Europe got taken care of." He looked bemused, like crazy people threatening software executives was out of the ordinary, which I suppose it was.

"You helped with that? He mentioned something to me about it."

"We did some legwork in France for that one. It was tricky because of the legal differences in the two countries. This last one was pretty easy, though."

"Last one?" I regarded him over the rim of the

mug.

"Yeah, digging up dirt on that guy who supposedly died. It took a while but we finally got a lead on him. He did a good job covering his tracks, but he disappeared so long ago almost all records were gone."

I nodded automatically, my thoughts whirling. Bell had been investigating Peter all along? He had proof that Peter was alive? Then what was this whole charade about? What was all this about finding proof from my father?

"We couldn't prove it was murder, though. That really pissed off T.K."

I jerked my mind back to the conversation. "What? I'm sorry. I don't understand."

"That girl in California. Her death was odd but we couldn't dig up any proof that the missing guy had anything to do with it."

"Girl in California?"

"The girlfriend." Bob got to his feet and headed for the back door. "Somebody's here."

I hadn't even heard the car pull in the drive, but Bob was at the back door, his hand hovering near the gun in the holster at the small of his back—a holster I hadn't even seen until now. I gaped at him when he opened the door, looked out quickly then held the door wider for Bell to enter. Like me, he wore black jeans and he'd swapped his suit for a dark blue shirt under a light gray sports jacket.

"I'm glad you changed, too," he said when he saw me. "I wasn't sure if I needed the suit or not."

"Mom wouldn't care what we wore," I said, picking up my bag from the table. "She'd want us to be comfortable." I smiled at Bob. "I'm glad to see I'm leaving Mom's cat in capable hands."

"I'll make sure he's taken care of. You guys take care of yourselves." Bob watched us leave then closed the door. I heard the lock snick shut behind us.

Bell was still driving the big sedan. "Thanks for doing all the chauffeur duty today," I said after slipping into the car.

"Thank you for including me." He drove south to Stuart Street then east, taking a route around the south edge of town rather than through the main streets.

I tried to think of a roundabout way to talk about what Bob told me then I decided to just be blunt. Hell, what did I have to lose? I was tired of secrets and tired of dancing around the truth, whatever that may be. "Bob told me that you had your security group investigate Peter. He said they found him for you."

Bell's mouth twisted in a wry smile. "I knew the truth would get out sooner or later. I was hoping it would be later."

"Why? Why all of this?" I raised my hands to encompass the last four days. "You knew Peter was alive. Why go through this whole game to pretend to look for proof?"

"This isn't a good time to tell you the whole thing." Bell slowed the car, easy to do because we were nearing a school and the speed limit changed anyway. "I'll tell you what I can and you'll just have to trust me for the rest."

"Trust you? After you've lied to me? I don't think so, Bell."

"Look. I had to flush Peter out into the open. We don't have any proof about the murder. That's what I want the proof for." He was speaking fast, words tumbling over each other.

"Is that the royal 'we'?" I demanded. "What murder? When?"

"Tina Lilly's murder. Jamie Lim's murder. Your mother."

"What?" I leaned back against the car door as though putting distance between us would make his talk more intelligible. "Jamie Lim? My mother?"

"I don't have time to give you all the details. Peter tried to blackmail me. My legal team contacted the police in California. During their investigation, they started to suspect—"

"He tried to blackmail you? He told me you were blackmailing him!"

"You talked to him? When? Is he here?" Bell shot me anxious glances, slowing the car more. A car behind us honked and he pulled to the curb, putting the car into park and turning to me. "When did you talk to him?"

"He called me yesterday and I saw him this morning, outside the house. He's going to be at the cemetery. He told me to bring all the proof we had about him. He said he'd expose you as a blackmailer if I didn't."

"You don't have any proof," Bell said flatly. "There really isn't any, nothing admissible in a court of law, at least."

"I know that. He said he was sure that Dad had proof. That's why he went through the house. I mean, I assume it was him."

Bell sighed heavily. "Your parents took money from Sylvia, years ago. Your mother felt guilty and wanted to make amends so she contacted Sylvia. I don't know how she got the address, but—"

"The Christmas card," I said. "Lightly showed her the Christmas card, remember?"

Bell nodded slowly. "That must be it. Anyway, your mother wanted to repay the money. It was tearing her up that they took illegal money. I tracked down Peter and that's when Peter tried to blackmail me." Bell's mouth twisted in a grim smile. "After all, I'm worth millions, right?"

"But what could he blackmail you about?"

Bell looked down at the steering wheel, struggling with some inner decision then he said, "I knew that Peter was still alive. Your mother loaned me money to get started in business. When I asked her where she got it, she told me. It was what remained after your father's medical expenses." He looked at me, his pale green eyes unflinching. "So technically I was an accessory to his fraud. And so was your mother."

"Holy crapola," I breathed.

"Why didn't you tell me about Peter?" Bell said. "Damn it, Wendy, didn't it occur to you that I can hire the best legal minds in the world to handle him? Why did you pay attention to anything he said? No matter what he does, I can have it handled."

"I didn't think about it. I just wanted to protect you." I frowned, perplexed. "Why wouldn't you tell me what was going on?"

"Hold on." Bell pulled back the right lapel of his sports coat and spoke into it. "Hey. We have a problem." He saw my astonished face and opened his jacket even wider, so I could see the small electronic gadget barely visible in the hem of the lining.

I stared at him, my mouth open. I'd seen enough movies to know he was wearing a wire.

Chapter 17

"What the hell is that?" I demanded. "Are you—?"

Bell held up a hand, his eyes narrowed in concentration. I fumed in silence, alternately glaring at him and at the innocent world outside the car.

"Okay, but I don't like it," he finally snapped. "Get them in place now. I'll do what I can to stall. This had better not get fucked up." He looked at me. "I'm working with the L.A. police, who are also working with the local police. There isn't time to explain everything. Your parents took money from Peter and Sylvia. Your mom wanted to pay it back, but she didn't know how to. She asked me to find Peter for her. In digging up Peter, I dug up Tina's death and Jamie Lim's death. He died six years after Peter disappeared, killed by a hit-and-run driver."

"Lim knew Peter was alive?" I murmured.

Bell nodded. "I think Sylvia and Peter paid him to keep his mouth shut but he asked for more money. Instead of paying him, they killed him."

"And Tina? Why her?"

"I'm not sure." His hands tightened on the steering wheel. "I think Sylvia got wind about what I was doing and she or Peter visited your mother. When your mother got sick—" He drew in a deep breath. "I wondered if I somehow led Peter to her."

"They visited…" My words faded when I realized

what he was implying. "You're saying one of them killed her?"

He nodded. "I'm guessing, but I think they found out that your mother didn't have definitive proof. All she could do was tell the authorities what she knew. And I think that's why they tried to kill her." He drew in a deep breath. "I've been wondering if I somehow led them to her. I've wondered if it's because of me that she—"

I put my hand on his arm. "Don't go down that road." I remembered Jason's voice. *It's personal for him.* If Bell thought he caused my mother any harm, he'd never forgive himself. "If anyone is to blame, it's Peter."

Bell nodded. "I know. I just hope we have a chance to make him pay for it." He glanced at the dashboard clock. "We have to get out there. Just follow my lead, okay? The police are going to get in place. Don't get far from me. If Peter shows up, stay away from him. They need a clear shot."

"What? Are you kidding? Aunt Jane is out there. This is a public place. You can't have a gunfight in Kensington Gardens!" I was breathless with outrage. This was insane. "Wait a minute. How can outside police be in town? They'd be spotted in a minute."

Bell put the car into gear and resumed driving. "It sure was useful that two reporters were on hand to rescue us from that car accident."

I gaped at him, again. "What?"

He smiled. "You're so trusting. That's why I was sure you could flush Peter out of the woodwork. He would never suspect you."

"Me flush Peter out..." I leaned against the car

door again, this time from shock. When I could finally speak again, I whispered, "Why you? Why did you get involved?"

His hands tightened on the steering wheel. "Peter made your mother's life miserable and if my suspicions are correct, he caused her stroke. It was time for payback."

"What do you mean? She never said anything to me about it."

"She wouldn't. She didn't want you to know. All these years she kept it a secret that she took money. She was ashamed they had to do it."

"But—but—"

"I can't explain it all now." Bell took my hand without removing his eyes from the road. "Just trust me, Wendy. Please."

"You just told me I was too trusting. Which is it?"

Bell smiled briefly. "I've never deliberately hurt you. I won't start now." He drove to the gates of the cemetery and we slowed again, this time to accommodate the narrow, twisting road winding through the place. "Try to act normally and stay close to me."

"Act normally? There are police coming, my mother might have been murdered, you're sure Peter is a murderer, and my mother's inurnment ceremony is about to begin. There's nothing normal about this!"

He squeezed my hand. "I'm sorry. You weren't supposed to get involved, at least not like this."

I tore my hand away from his. "You know, if one more person tries to protect poor little me I'm going to haul off and hit him. I can take care of myself, Bell."

He ignored my tantrum, staring ahead. "I'm sure

nothing will happen until the service is over. Just stay close to me."

I took in a deep breath, trying to calm the boiling excitement percolating in the pit of my stomach. My hands trembled when I picked up my purse from the floor where I had set it. I felt the reassuring weight of Dad's gun, and my nervousness immediately ceased. It was a reminder of him and my mother and their strength and courage all those years. If they could face illness and death with such dignity, the least I could do was try to emulate them.

Bell pulled in behind the funeral sedan, which was parked on the verge of the narrow drive. This part of the cemetery had mostly headstones denoting graves rather than in-ground markers. Two large rectangular mausoleums were about thirty feet away on my left, important looking structures on top of a gentle hill. Big trees shaded them on the small knoll.

My parents would bring us to the cemetery to visit David's grave and the graves of my grandparents, all clustered in this area. We kids used to wander around and I remember peering at the mausoleums, which housed a husband who was a key figure in the settling of the town and his second wife.

Not far from them was a headstone of the man's first wife, almost as imposing as the granite mini-buildings. It had an enormous black angel poised on top of it, peering down at the second wife's mausoleum. When we were kids, we used to joke that it was really the first wife keeping an eye on the second one. Aunt Jane had told us the man's family disapproved of the second marriage, so this was his children's way of making sure the second wife knew.

A fanciful story and one that flitted through my head while I emerged from the car. Bell held out his arm and I slipped my hand through it while we walked through the warm grass to the tent. The day had turned humid and still, so quiet I could hear the faint buzz of farm equipment in the distance.

The funeral people had erected a small tent over our family headstones. It was just big enough for the minister, Jane, Bell, and me, providing welcome shade as well as shelter from the misty rain that was starting. The minister stood near the small spot of cleared earth where Mom's remains were already placed.

I took a seat next to Aunt Jane, sitting on a wooden folding chair which rested on a thick carpet spread on the grass near the headstone. Bell sat next to me, his gaze sweeping around the area before settling on the minister.

Mom and Dad shared a headstone. On the right were smaller ones for Mike, David, and John. The boys' headstones were simple, with just their birth and death dates. I think, at the time, it was all my parents could do. The grief at losing a child precluded any sentiments on their markers. Mom and Dad had chosen phrases for theirs.

George Llewellyn Davis. "He is not dead, he is just away."

Mary Ansell Davis. "I return to the dream from which I was born."

I blinked back tears. When Dad died, Mom had her inscription engraved at the same time his was done. All that was needed to make it complete was her death date. My whole family was here, gathered around me. I took Aunt Jane's hand when the enormity of that sank in.

Everyone I grew up with, everyone who knew me from childhood, was here.

Bell took my other hand, raising it to his lips and kissing it then releasing it. His touch reminded me that I wasn't right. I'd known him since I was a small child and although we were separated for more years than we'd been together, I still had someone close to me who was a part of my past. It was reassuring and strengthening.

The minister spoke for a few minutes, quoting scripture then saying a little homily about two souls reunited in heaven, two spirits who would never be separated again. It was perfectly true of my parents. They were two people attuned to each other, truly happy together. I felt a spark of happiness at the thought my mother would finally be with Dad after all that time apart, and my brothers would be with them. Now she'd be whole again.

"I visited Mary in the hospital several times," the minister said, closing his Bible and looking first at the headstone then at me. "Once you understood her method of communication, it was amazing how much talking we really did." He smiled at me, his eyes full of compassion. "She was so proud of her Wendy Darling and all she accomplished in her life. Mary was thankful for the many visits she had with her daughter and she grieved to think that Wendy would be sad at her death."

"I know that having her sister nearby was a comfort to Mary," he said to Jane, who nodded sadly, her hand still clasped with mine. "She felt she was always surrounded by love and she knew her daughter would have that love and support later, when she most needed it."

His gaze shifted to Bell. "Mary knew Tom would also do all he could to help Wendy if she needed it. Tom was a good friend to Mary, not just out of gratitude for all that Mary and George did for him, but out of love for them. A true friend is a rare and wondrous gift, and Mary knew it."

The minister put his hand on the gravestone, giving it a final, gentle caress. "We say good-bye today, but you will always have them in your hearts to guide you and support you in the days ahead. Try not to be sad but understand that sometimes death can be a gift. It was that for your mother, Wendy. It was a release from her pain and a chance to be with her beloved husband once again." He nodded and stepped away from us, moving to the car parked in front of Bell's.

We three sat silently for a long moment then Aunt Jane stood and went to the grave, touching the headstone. "I always envied your mother. She had such a full life with all the kids and she loved George so much. I didn't have that kind of relationship with my husband. Your parents did have a one-of-a-kind marriage, I think."

I went to her side. "I never realized it, I suppose. I think I thought that's how all marriages worked. It wasn't until I was older that I knew how special it was."

"I think I'll go back now." Jane dabbed at her eyes with a handkerchief, lace-edged and feminine like her pale blue dress and shoes. "I need to be alone for a while. How about you? Do you want to come with me?"

I wanted to go. God knows I did, but I had to face Peter. I hugged her. "I need some time with Mom and Dad." I walked with her to the car and the minister, who stood nearby.

Jane paused before she got into the passenger seat. "Don't let your grief interfere with your judgment, dear."

I glanced back at the grave. Bell was there, staring into the distance. "I won't. I know this is all just temporary. I know it isn't real."

Jane shook her head, white hair as tidy as ever in a braided bun. "Nonsense. That's exactly what I meant. You're over-thinking this, Wendy. For once in your life, let your emotions rule the day."

"That's crazy, Aunt Jane."

"What's crazy is your blindness to what you feel. I've known you all our life, Wendy Davis, and I've never known you to act unless you've carefully thought through all possible consequences. Sometimes you think so long you miss an opportunity."

"Nonsense," I mimicked. "I don't know what you mean."

"You lost out on a scholarship to UCLA because you were worried about moving away. You didn't take that job in Atlanta because it wasn't quite right. All your life you've taken the safe path." She looked past me. "He's known and he's unknown, so you're taking the safe path and you're pushing him away."

Jane slid into the passenger seat with the agility of a woman half her age. "You're over-thinking this, Wendy. Go with your gut. I'll see you later. Take your time." She pulled the door closed, leaving me standing in the mist.

I watched the car leave then I walked slowly through the wet grass, the cool blades tickling my ankles. Bell turned to me, his eyes darting here and there. I was so exhausted it took a minute before I remembered why he was so anxious. I watched the minister's car make a turn at the junction in the road then I continued walking to the gravestone, my mind in a spin.

I touched the damp, cool granite. This day was a series of flips and dips, culminating in Bell's story about working with the police. On the one hand, I was happy to have something to divert me from my grief, but paradoxically, I wished I could just have my grief and embrace it. I was tired of being distracted.

"Would you mind leaving me alone for a minute?" I asked Bell.

"Are you kidding, Wendy Darling?" a taunting voice said from somewhere to my left. "This is perfect." Peter moved out of the shadows behind the husband's mausoleum, a gun in his hand.

I jumped, almost knocking over the tent. Bell moved closer to me but stopped when Peter gestured with the gun. I looked around nervously. Now would be a good time for any cops to leap out and arrest someone. It appeared we were alone, though.

"I finally have you where I want you, Tom." Peter's gun was aimed directly at Bell's heart. Even though he was yards away, I was sure he would kill Bell if he shot. "I can finally kill you, you blackmailing son of a bitch."

"You shouldn't toss around insults, Peter. They might come back to land on you." Bell looked and sounded perfectly relaxed, as though we were all just chatting about old times instead of having a gun aimed at us.

"Blackmail?" I tried to step back but the ground

was uneven and I wobbled.

"Stay put," Peter snapped. "Yes, blackmail. Your father told Tom he saw me that night. Tom went to my mother and she paid him off and she paid off your father. Then later, when he needed more money, Tom tried to get more out of us. We didn't pay, though. We were at a stalemate. If he revealed what he knew, he'd be arrested for obstruction of justice."

"And if you revealed what you did, you'd be arrested for murder." Bell shrugged. "Nice story, Peter. Too bad it isn't real." He looked at me, his eyes boring into mine. "Play along," he said softly while Peter moved down the small hill toward us. "Play your part."

I swallowed hard. What part was I supposed to play? I didn't know anymore. "You knew?" I turned on Bell with supposed anger. "You knew Peter was alive all this time?"

"I didn't know for sure. Your father implied he knew something, but he didn't tell me what. That's why I wanted the notebooks."

"Notebooks?" Peter's brow furrowed with puzzlement. "What notebooks?"

"You didn't get them when you robbed the house. I had them." Bell glanced from me to Peter, turning so his right side—the one with the electronic wire—was facing more toward Peter. "I had the notebooks. That's the proof about what happened that night." Bell hesitated and now he looked puzzled. "There was one thing in the code I didn't understand. George said he saw you and another man."

"Another man?" I blinked in startled surprise. "Jamie Lim?"

Peter laughed harshly. "No, not Lim. Not that

night, at least." He moved closer to us, now just a few yards separating us. "You mean there was other stuff in that safety deposit box? We searched the whole fucking house and didn't find anything."

Bell nodded. "George's notebooks."

"You blackmailed him?" I asked Bell. "You knew?"

Bell shifted, turning slightly to face me directly. "Sylvia Barry paid your father twenty-five thousand to keep quiet about seeing Peter that night. Your father used the money for your college and for his medical expenses, but the cancer advanced so quickly, they— your parents—decided not to continue treatment. Your mother saved any money that was left and invested it. Later, when I was just starting out, your mother offered to loan it to me. I didn't realize where it came from but I suspected."

I looked from Bell to Peter in mute shock.

"About five years ago, she told me," Bell said. "I volunteered to find Peter and pay it all back, with interest. It took me a while, but I did it. I handled it."

That's what Bell did, I thought. He handled things. "You paid him off?" I spoke over my shoulder because Bell was now slightly behind me, moving around me on my left. "Then it was true? They gave my parents money to keep quiet?"

"Your father was sick. Insurance wouldn't cover his expenses. They had no choice." Bell's voice was flat, non-accusatory.

"Your mother developed a conscience. She wanted to tell the authorities I was still alive. It wasn't enough that Tom paid back the money. She wanted me to pay it back, too." Peter's low, sharp voice told me how angry he was. When Peter got mad, his voice seemed to drop an octave and became soft, like a snake rustling through grass.

"I argued with her," Bell said. "I told her to leave well enough alone. What was past was past and couldn't be changed. But she felt so terrible about it. And then she got sick." His gaze flickered to Peter. "Supposedly."

"This was all a lie?" I threw up my hands in despair. "All of this?"

"Of course not. I still care for you." Bell said it almost in dismissal, just like—yes—just like talking to an idiot child.

I swear to God if he wasn't standing behind me and if I could have put my hands on my gun at that moment I would have shot him. As it was, I turned to slap him. That's when he stepped around me and raised a gun, aiming it directly at Peter.

I edged away from Bell, casting furtive glances around the cemetery. There was no one in sight. Where were the police? Why didn't someone interrupt? The weather and the fading daylight gave the scene the appearance of a movie set with swirls of smoky-looking air drifting on the faint breeze. If this kept up, we'd be hard pressed to see each other in the next half hour or so.

If we lived that long.

Peter didn't appear worried by Bell's gun. He shifted his aim, his gun aimed at me. I held up my hands in a *whoa, calm down* gesture. "Quit moving, Wendy," Peter said. "Stay put."

"I don't want to be caught in the crossfire."

"You don't want to stay by the side of the man you

love?" Peter took a step closer, his gaze flicking from me to Bell. "I'm surprised at you, Wendy. You always struck me as the kind of woman who would stand by her man."

"That tells you how much you know about me." I inched to the right, away from Bell and from Peter, who approached slowly.

"Drop the gun, Peter." Bell's aim was steady and his gaze didn't shift from Peter.

"No, Tom. You drop your gun."

I whirled when I heard the voice behind me. A tall woman stepped out from behind the wife's mausoleum, her gun pointed directly at me. She was stylishly dressed in a floral print dress, chunky-heeled shoes, and a perky white hat that showed just a hint of her blonde hair under its white brim. It was hard to guess her age. She might have been thirty or seventy. I glanced at her hands. Mom always said you could tell a woman by her hands. I revised my estimate of her age upward, to sixty or so.

Bell turned slowly to his right so he could easily look at the woman and at Peter. "Hello, Sylvia."

Chapter 18

The woman smiled. "Hello, Tom. Long time, no see."

"Sylvia? Sylvia Barry?" I stared at the woman, trying to see the slender girl-mother from decades earlier. All I saw now was a hardened, sophisticated woman with no hint of sympathy or compassion on her well-sculpted face. A face, I suspected, that had seen its share of plastic surgery in the not-too-distant past. "What are you doing here?"

"I thought Peter might need some help." She walked carefully down the slope toward us, a small gun in her hand.

While she was distracted, I shot furtive glances around us. Where in hell were the police? Peter was looking anxiously at his mother and Bell, who hadn't lowered his gun one inch. In fact, I realized, I was the only one here who wasn't overtly armed. Holy crapola. I was in the middle of a damn firefight.

I inched backward, aiming for the carpeted area under the tent. I had a vague idea that if I could drop to the ground there, the wooden folding chairs might provide some measure of protection. A stupid thought, perhaps, but it was the best I could come up.

Bell appeared calm, totally prepared for the fact that two people were pointing guns at us. Peter was still turned so he could aim at me and Sylvia's gun was unwavering, pointed at Bell. "You thought he needed help or you were afraid he'd screw it up?" Bell asked.

Peter's mouth thinned into an angry line and I knew Bell's little jab hit home. "Who was the mastermind behind it all, Peter?" I inched back more. "Was it you or her?"

Sylvia was ten feet away, her dark brown eyes cold. "I thought of it, of course. We had to do something. All our plans were unraveling." She glanced at her son, who looked miffed at this dismissal of his involvement. "I didn't think it would work, but Peter was right. He said you'd all act exactly the way you all did. And it worked. Now give us the proof, and no one gets hurts. That's all we need." Her hand with the gun wavered and I swallowed hard, praying she knew how to handle it.

"Unraveling?" Bell frowned. "What was unraveling?"

Sylvia looked at me when she answered. "Your father saw Peter and his father that night."

"What? Your father came home?" I looked at Peter and he nodded. Then I turned to Bell, expecting to see shock on his face, too. What I saw was satisfaction. "You knew?"

He glanced at me but returned his gaze immediately to Sylvia. "I debugged the program, remember?"

The program. The pseudo-code my father wrote describing that night. I only skimmed it, so I wasn't sure what was in there. Peter and his father? My eyes widened in disbelief.

Sylvia saw my astonishment. "Honestly, Wendy. For a supposedly intelligent girl, you're pretty stupid."

I didn't take offense at her comment, but I did take offense at the condescending way she said it. I was getting tired of people treating me like a simpleton. "I may be stupid but at least I'm not wanted for murder," I snapped.

"Neither am I." Her composure didn't waver. "No one can prove anything."

"Unless we exhume the body and run a DNA test," Bell said.

Choking silence covered us all. "Perhaps," Sylvia said. "But it won't come to that, will it, Tom?"

"I don't understand." I said it to Bell. "Peter's father returned home?"

"We were one month away from declaring him legally dead." Peter had moved and now all my little maneuverings were in vain. He once again had a clear shot at me. "We kept up the life insurance policy for him and for me. Didn't you wonder why we were so poor, Wendy?"

I shook my head mutely. Both Peter and Bell were poor growing up, but I never gave it much thought. Both were from single-parent households and I just assumed that was why. As with so much, my assumptions were wrong.

"That son of a bitch came back a month before I stood to inherit one million dollars." Sylvia's gaze remained fixed on my face but I saw her dart little glances at Bell, as though gauging his reaction. "He came back and that's when Peter devised his plan to conveniently die and put the blame squarely on you, little Wendy, the darling of Kensington."

I tried to laugh but it came out more like a choked croak. "Bullshit," I managed.

"Oh, it was true. You didn't see it, but everyone else did. You were Princess of this and Queen of that. Head of the Honor Society, President of the student council, head cheerleader, leader of the Glee Club." Sylvia waved her free hand dramatically. "Whatever contest you entered, you won. Whatever office you ran for, you won. You were so sincere, so sweet, so—"

"Gullible," Peter finished for her. "I knew you'd blame yourself if I declared my undying love for you."

"And you knew the police wouldn't pursue a verdict of suicide if it meant implicating Wendy in his death," Bell said. "You were banking a lot on her popularity and the police being sympathetic to her."

"Not just her." Sylvia's voice dripped with venom. "Her fucking parents, too. The perfect couple. Handsome, so pretty, so well-matched. Children flocked to their house because they welcomed everyone. It was *the* place for kids to hang out because her father was cool and her mother was so sweet and patient. He did charity legal work for Viet Nam vets. She served on every volunteer committee in town." Sylvia's face twisted into a mask of scorn. "They were so well-loved that no one in town would want to besmirch their names, especially something that could harm their children. After all, they had been through tragedy, losing their oldest son. Everyone felt sorry for them. No, we were safe and we knew it."

"All we had to do was kill my father, rough up his body so it wouldn't be recognizable, let him rot for a while, then toss him in the river." Peter smiled at the memory.

"There wasn't any DNA testing back then. Besides, I identified the body." Sylvia gestured with the gun and

Bell moved closer to me. "No one questioned it."

"Mary Davis told me," Bell said. "They were desperate for money. Then, later, she was afraid to tell the police what she knew. She was afraid she might be implicated and then what would happen to Wendy?"

"We bought them off," Sylvia said. "They needed money for college expenses and for his health care."

"Why didn't they tell me?" I whispered. "They could have told me. Mom didn't have to keep it a secret all those years."

"Because no one wanted to hurt you," Peter sneered. "Little Wendy Darling. Nobody wants to hurt Wendy."

Days of pent-up confusion, anger, and grief started to boil in my gut. I wanted to throw up. I wanted to hit somebody. I wanted to scream. "Fuck you, Peter," I spat.

His eyes widened. "Oh. Little Wendy is angry. Tsk."

"I found out about it later," Bell said. "Your mother felt so guilty. I offered to find Peter and pay it all back."

"And that's when we realized there might be a complication." Sylvia raised the gun slightly higher. Now it was pointed directly at my heart. "Your mother's conscience was bothering her. And she involved Tom Bell."

"She didn't know about the murder." Bell glanced at me, his green eyes intent and reassuring. "All your parents knew was that Sylvia and Peter defrauded the insurance company, claiming Peter died."

I shook my head. "Didn't Mom and Dad wonder who it was in the river?"

Bell's mouth tightened into a flat line. "Sylvia explained that perfectly. She told your parents it was a veteran she worked with, someone who was terminally ill and wanted to commit suicide, someone in pain."

Sylvia shot me a pitying look. "Your parents believed it. They wanted to believe it because they needed the money. I told your father it was assisted suicide. The man overdosed and Peter and I disposed of his body to save his family the grief. Your parents bought it. They even sympathized. I can see where you got your gullibility, Wendy."

That was third or fourth time someone called me gullible. I held on to my temper, forcing myself to think rationally. "What about Tina?"

Sylvia stiffened. "What do you know about her?"

"I—Totts—Totts said that Tina died. I thought maybe she was with you." I stuttered out an explanation, realizing my mistake too late.

Peter looked momentarily sad. "I hated to do that to Tina. All I wanted was for her to join me." He shot a venomous look at his mother.

"We discussed that, Peter," she said calmly. "Tina couldn't be trusted. It was better we didn't have to worry about her."

"You killed her?" I asked incredulously. "Good Lord, don't you have a conscience?"

"It's all about survival," Sylvia said. "We had almost two million dollars at stake between two insurance policies. I wasn't going to let anything or anyone jeopardize that."

"What are you going to do? Kill us both? That might look a little suspicious, don't you think?" Where were the police? Didn't they have enough information?

What else did they need?

Bell grabbed my arm. "What are you going to do, Sylvia? It's over."

"We want the proof." She gestured with the gun. "Once we get the proof, everybody goes home and nobody gets hurt."

"That's crap," I blurted. "There isn't any proof."

Her eyes narrowed, the long and obviously fake lashes fluttering with her action. "What? Why would they—" She looked at me then at Bell, who still held his gun and had me in a tight grip. "What's going on?"

"Leave her out of this." Bell shoved me and I stumbled into one of the folding chairs. "She doesn't know anything. Let her go and I'll give you all the proof."

Sylvia tilted her head slightly to one side. "I don't think so," she said slowly. "Peter, get Wendy. We need to split them up. Maybe if we have a hostage, he'll cooperate."

"I told you I'd cooperate." Bell stepped forward and lowered his gun, crouching to set it on the ground. "I will. Trust me."

I wanted to laugh. Instead I cowered and let my handbag slip off my shoulder.

"Get up, Wendy," Sylvia snapped. "You're going with Peter."

I knelt to pick up my bag, pretending to overbalance and fall forward. I dug my hand into the center section of the purse, pulled out the gun, flicked off the safety, stood, and aimed. "Bell!"

He turned. His eyes opened wide when he saw me aiming at him.

"Now who's predictable?"

Peter laughed behind me.

I whirled around and shot. The bullet went wide. I knew it would. I didn't have time to aim and I've never shot at a person before. But it did what I wanted. It surprised them. As soon as I fired, I dropped to the ground, crashing into the chairs, and bringing them down on top of me. I struggled to free myself and peered out from the confining wood.

Bell and Peter were fighting for Peter's gun, tussling around on the ground. Two men were running toward us, racing over the knoll where the mausoleums sat. Two other men ran toward us from the opposite direction, near the cemetery entrance. Each had a gun drawn and each looked like they knew how to use it.

I flailed amongst the chair legs, finally righting myself enough to get to my hands and knees. Someone grabbed my hair and my head was jerked back. I stared into the barrel of a gun.

"You little bitch," Sylvia spat. "I'll kill you for this." I struggled to my feet, propelled by her painful grip. "What does he know?" Sylvia shook me and I swear I felt hair being pulled out by the roots. "What's going on? What did he do?"

"It's all recorded," I gasped, grabbing for her hands. She pressed the gun against the side of my head, near my ear. "He went to the police."

She drew in her breath in a long hiss. "What about the proof? Your mother had proof."

"There is none." Tears streamed down my face while I struggled weakly, trying to break free without getting shot. "There never was any. Bell lied."

"That bastard." She released me and I dropped like rock, crashing back into the chairs. My vision blurred and for an instant all I saw were exploding stars. I rolled onto my back and looked up, groggily.

Sylvia straddled my body, her gun arm straight out and pointed at Bell, who stood over Peter. I grabbed for her leg. She kicked out, hitting me in the stomach. I ignored the pain and tried to pull her off balance. I glimpsed men running toward us but they were far away. Bell was only a few feet away. Sylvia wouldn't miss him.

I got to my knees, grabbed a wooden chair, and swung it with all my might upward. It caught Sylvia in the back. She twisted, falling sideways with her gun still in her hand. For one frozen moment, I stared into the barrel again. Then the gun went off and I ducked.

Men swarmed over us, two landing on Sylvia and one landing partially on me. I tried to get out of the melee but was caught up in the churning tangle of arms and legs. Sharp pain hit my face then I was free, staggering to my feet and wandering a couple of paces only to fall, landing hard on my butt.

I peered around blearily. One man had hold of Peter, his arms held behind his back while another man handcuffed him. Two other men held Sylvia face-down on the ground, one with his hand on her head and the other with a hand in the small of her back. Even with two big guys holding her, she still squirmed.

"Wendy. You're hurt. Wendy." Bell raced toward me and skidded to a stop, landing just as hard next to me as I'd landed a second before. He knelt in front of me and stared intently into my face. "Are you okay? Were you shot?"

I looked down at my clothing which appeared grass-stained but unbloodied. "I don't think so. I think

I'm okay." Then a stunning pain lanced through my left cheekbone. "I think I got hit in the face."

He gently touched my jaw, moving my head carefully to the right. "You'll have a black eye tomorrow. Are you sure you're okay otherwise?"

I blew out a shaky breath. "I think so. What the hell happened?"

"The police finally arrived. They had to wait to make their move until they had Sylvia on tape confessing to killing her husband. They had to stay out of sight until then so they had a long way to run to get here."

"Was it true? Any of it?" I shook my head, wincing when pain exploded into my left eye socket. "My parents took hush money from Peter and Sylvia, who killed Peter's father and two other people, all for a million dollars."

Bell nodded. "That pretty much sums it up. Your mother loaned me money to get started in business, and when I tried to pay her back, she told me about it. That's when I tracked down Peter and—"

"And the police got involved and now here we are."

The voice was above me. "You?" I asked.

Billy Juko, the so-called reporter, grinned at me. "Yep. We needed a cover and T.K. Bell's romance with his old high school sweetheart was a great cover."

I switched my attention to Bell. "Really? Was any of that true?"

He gave me a wide-eyed look. "It was all true, Wendy. All of it."

I narrowed my eyes and glared at him then winced when the action made my left eye water with pain. "I'm not sure I believe it." I spied Dad's gun on the ground and picked it up, flicking the safety back on.

"I'll take that," another voice said. I peered up groggily and found Murphy Black, the big reporter, smiling down at me.

"You're a cop, too?" I asked, reaching out a hand.

"Yep." He pulled me to my feet. "Thanks for the help. You did great."

"All I did was be myself." I ran a hand through my hair, coming up with a few snarled tangles that fell out.

"That's all you had to do," Bell said. "Just be yourself." He stood and put an arm around my shoulders and I leaned against him, happy for the support. "Where did you get a gun?"

"Dad had one." It was heavy in my hand but I expected that. Every time I picked up a gun, it surprised me how heavy it was. I handed it to Murphy, who inspected the safety then handed it to another man. "He taught us all how to shoot."

"I didn't know that."

I smiled. "I guess there are some things about Wendy Darling that are still a secret, then, aren't there?"

"I guess so." He spoke the words slowly, reluctantly.

"Not all things can be programmed. You need to adjust your app for that. You need to plan for the unexpected. Not everyone is predictable, you know."

He grinned. "I told you that I wanted you to help me design the next version. It looks like there's a lot of work for us to do."

"Don't over-think," I said. "Go with your gut."

He put his arms around me. "Are you sure?"

I raised my face to his. "Quit asking questions, Bell."

A word about the author...

J L Wilson writes romantic mysteries with a bit of a twist to keep you guessing. She also writes reincarnation love stories as well as dystopian futuristic stories. Yes, she does keep busy.

Catch up with her at www.jayellwilson.com.

~*~

For a list of "who's who" in this book, see http://bit.ly/character_lists—some of them might surprise you!

Thank you for purchasing
this publication of The Wild Rose Press, Inc.

If you enjoyed the story, we would appreciate your
letting others know by leaving a review.

For other wonderful stories,
please visit our on-line bookstore at
www.thewildrosepress.com.

For questions or more information
contact us at
info@thewildrosepress.com.

The Wild Rose Press, Inc.
www.thewildrosepress.com

Stay current with The Wild Rose Press, Inc.

Like us on Facebook

https://www.facebook.com/TheWildRosePress

And Follow us on Twitter
https://twitter.com/WildRosePress